Hill, Donna (Donna O.).
My love at last.

My Love at Last

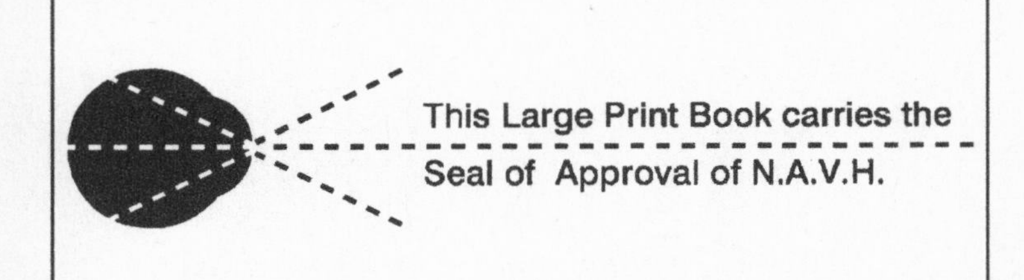
This Large Print Book carries the
Seal of Approval of N.A.V.H.

A SAG HARBOR VILLAGE NOVEL, BOOK 3

MY LOVE AT LAST

DONNA HILL

THORNDIKE PRESS
A part of Gale, Cengage Learning

GALE
CENGAGE Learning

Farmington Hills, Mich • San Francisco • New York • Waterville, Maine
Meriden, Conn • Mason, Ohio • Chicago

A Sag Harbor Village Novel #3.
Thorndike Press, a part of Gale, Cengage Learning.

Thorndike Press® Large Print African-American.
The text of this Large Print edition is unabridged.
Other aspects of the book may vary from the original edition.
Set in 16 pt. Plantin.

LIBRARY OF CONGRESS CATALOGING-IN-PUBLICATION DATA

Hill, Donna (Donna O.)
My love at last / Donna Hill. — Large print edition.
pages cm. — (A Sag Harbor village novel ; 3) (Thorndike Press large print African-American)
ISBN 978-1-4104-8284-6 (hardback) — ISBN 1-4104-8284-7 (hardcover)
1. African Americans—Fiction. 2. Large type books. I. Title.
PS3558.I3864M9 2015
813'.54—dc23 2015030993

Published in 2015 by arrangement with Harlequin Books S. A.

Printed in Mexico
1 2 3 4 5 6 7 19 18 17 16 15

This novel is lovingly dedicated in memory of my dearest friend, confidant and mentor Gwynne Forster.

CHAPTER 1

Tall, dark, sleek. He stood framed in the doorway. He was clad in all black that only served to emphasize the sensual intensity that wafted around him like musical notes. She watched him, hypnotized by the way his long fingers wrapped around the glass that he lifted to his mouth. He swallowed and could taste the warm amber liquid as it slid down his throat. Sensing his prey, he turned his head slowly in her direction. She should have looked away but she didn't move. His dark, deep-set eyes sucked her into a vortex of heat that raised the hair on the back of her neck. His mouth, that full, lush mouth, flickered ever so slightly. His eyes settled on her over the rim of his glass and he tipped it subtly in her direction. Her nipples puckered against the fabric of her bra. She shifted her body, but she couldn't tear her gaze away. A woman crossed her line of vision and played up to him, touching his arm with familiarity, laughing and smiling. She linked her arm through his and they walked out to the back lawn, where the party was in full swing.

Olivia Gray sucked in air, catching the breath that had escaped her. She felt warm all over and her throat was as dry as if she'd slept with her mouth open. She plucked a glass of champagne off the tray of a passing waiter and took a much-needed swallow.

"Having a good time?"

Olivia blinked, turned toward the voice of her hostess. "Yes, Melanie, thanks for inviting me."

Melanie Harte, owner of The Platinum Society, an elite matchmaking service, was legendary in Sag Harbor for her amazing parties. This one was no exception. "I make it a point that all the newcomers to the Harbor feel welcome and get to know each other." Her gaze followed the direction of Olivia's. "His name is Connor Lawson," she said quietly, with a gleam of knowing in her light eyes.

Olivia flushed. "Who?"

Melanie's laughter tinkled like fine crystal. "I'm very good at what I do, Olivia, and I know a connection when I see one. The electricity between the two of you lit up the room." She stepped closer and turned to face Olivia. "I think that an introduction is in order. You both have a lot in common." She lifted her chin toward the back door. "Lydia won't hold his attention long. She's not his type."

"How do you know all this?"

Melanie sipped her champagne. "Do you want to meet him or not?"

Olivia's lips parted. "All right."

They crossed the expanse of the living room, with Melanie stopping every few feet to say a word or make introductions among her guests. She finally stepped outside, scanned the gathering on the lawn. The well-dressed guests lounged at the tables dotting the manicured grass or chatted in tight conversation groups.

"Over there," Melanie said. She walked in the direction of Connor, who was leaning against a willow tree listening to Lydia.

Olivia followed closely, casually looking about and casting a smile here and there to keep her mind off the next few steps, which would land her right in front of Connor Lawson.

"Connor." Melanie slid up to him and possessively draped her arm around his waist. "I see Lydia is monopolizing all of your time." She flashed a false smile at Lydia while she smoothly angled herself between the two of them. "How are you enjoying yourself, Lydia?"

"Wonderful as always."

"I do want to talk with you about a few things."

Lydia's finely arched brows rose in question. "Oh."

"Excuse my manners. Connor Lawson, this is Dr. Olivia Gray. She's here from New York on a research project. And you're working on the restoration of the homestead, right?"

"I am." He turned the full wattage of his maleness on Olivia.

Her breath hitched. The air around them crackled.

"What are you researching?" he asked her. He pulled her in with his bottomlessness voice.

"The origins of the African-American families of Sag Harbor." Her own sketchy beginnings might be buried here, but no one needed to know that.

Moonlight pinged the dark orbs of his eyes. "Perhaps we can compare notes."

"I think that's a great plan," Melanie said. "Why don't you two work out those details while Lydia and I talk about *that thing.*" She hooked her arm through Lydia's and ushered her away before she could form the words of protest.

Connor rolled his gaze toward Olivia, and she turned the energy right back on him. The corner of his mouth quirked into a grin. "You have a New York vibe."

"And what kind of vibe would that be?"

He took a swallow of his drink. "Sophisticated. Savvy. Sexy."

The bud between her legs twitched in response. "Do you say that to all the girls from New York?"

"Only the special ones."

Olivia raked her bottom lip with her teeth.

Connor studied the erotic move and wondered if she was intentionally trying to turn him on. It wouldn't take much. He'd felt the rise for her the instant he spotted her across the room.

"Melanie said you're doing restoration work. The Homestead?" she said, shifting the tone and direction of the conversation.

He slid his free hand into his pocket to keep from touching her. "One of the original string of cabins. Challenging work. There's a lot of history buried out there. Every day is a treasure hunt."

Olivia felt his energy and his passion from the pitch of his voice and the spark in his eyes. He loved what he did, and she knew that he was good at it. He would be good at anything he did.

"I'd love to see it . . . what you're working on. I'm sure it would help me with my own work."

"We'll have to work that out, and then you can tell me all about your research." His eyes snaked over her, teasing her flesh. Was her skin as silky as it looked encased in that body-hugging royal blue? His jaw clenched. And those legs . . . wrapped around his back.

She brought her glass to her lips. "What got you involved in restoration?"

"Long story." For the first time his steady gaze wavered. He shifted his body weight. "What about you? What kind of doctor are you?"

"Anthropologist."

His right brow flicked in admiration. "Beauty *and* brains."

Her black lashes lowered over her lids. "How long is your story?"

"Maybe I'll tell you about it over dinner."

Her brown eyes settled on his face. "Are you asking me out, Mr. Lawson?"

"All my friends call me Connor. And yes, in answer to your question, I'm asking you to join me for drinks and dinner."

Why did it sound like so much more, or was it only her libido talking?

"There you are. I've been looking all over for you."

Olivia glanced over her bare right shoulder and smiled. "Desiree. Sorry. Melanie whisked me away."

"I see you've met Connor." She stepped up to him and kissed his cheek. "I hope you haven't been using that naughty Lawson charm of yours on Olivia."

Connor grinned, baring a flash of even white teeth. "I never thought of myself as naughty. We were having a very intense business discussion." He slid his gaze toward Olivia. "Isn't that right?"

"All business."

Her lips pursed ever so slightly, and he had every intention of tasting them before the night was over.

Desiree looked from one to the other. "Hmm. Well, Lincoln and I are leaving soon," she said to Olivia. "Ready?"

"Oh . . . okay." Olivia made a move as if to leave.

"I'd be happy to drive you home if you aren't ready now."

Olivia flashed him a look. Did she need to be hemmed up with him in a car, with the irrational way her body was reacting to him? "If you're sure you don't mind?"

His eyes narrowed. "Looking forward to it."

"Then, I will see you two later," Desiree said. She squeezed Olivia's upper arm and wagged a warning finger at Connor. "Play nice."

"Always." He winked.

Desiree chuckled and went in search of her husband, Lincoln.

"You're staying at The Port?" Connor asked.

"Yes. I am."

"My cousin-in-law Layla runs the spa over there."

Olivia brightened as the pieces clicked in place. "You're related to Maurice and Layla?"

"Maurice is my first cousin."

"You get discounts on the massages?"

"No. But I give pretty good massages." Connor tipped his head to the side and looked at her from beneath a veil of thick lashes. "So I've been told."

Her heart thumped.

"Walk?"

She gave a slight shrug. "Sure."

He placed his hand at the small of her back, right above the rise of her very round derriere. He took a quick peek. *Lovely.*

She felt the heated imprint of his palm,

wanted it lower. Warmth spread between her inner thighs.

Connor guided her away from the house and across the slope toward the beach. The rushing sound of the ocean rolling toward the shore and beating against the rocks grew stronger.

"How long have you been here?" Connor asked.

"Just about three weeks."

"Surprised we haven't met sooner."

"I've been buried in notes and journals since I arrived. Desiree convinced me that I needed a break and got me invited here tonight."

"I'll have to thank Desiree."

"For what?"

"For realizing that you needed to take a break. Otherwise think of all the time wasted before we would've met."

Everything he said was an invitation. He kept opening the door, waiting for her to step through. She wouldn't be that easy. Not now. Not just yet. "What about you? How long have you been here?"

"Almost a year. I got commissioned to work on the restoration last summer."

"What are some of the other projects you've worked on?"

"Hmm, brownstones on Strivers Row,

theaters, African burial grounds in Manhattan . . ." He shrugged. "Things like that. What about you?"

"I've visited the burial grounds and examined the remains. It was quite surreal to realize who those people were . . . our ancestors," she said with quiet reverence. "How did you get started?"

He was thoughtful for a moment, looked skyward. "The incident that pushed me was when I took a trip to Goree Island in Senegal during my first year in college."

"Incredible place," she enthused. She stopped, bent down and took off her shoes. She looped the straps over her fingers.

Connor followed suit as they approached the sandy beach. "How long is your project?"

"Much of it depends on what I find." She tilted her head toward him for a moment, then looked away. The sand was warm beneath her feet. She flexed her toes, letting the grains run over and between them. "This feels good."

"What night are you free?"

"Free?"

"For drinks and dinner."

"Oh. Umm, Tuesday," she said randomly.

"Eight good for you." It wasn't really a question.

"Yes. Eight sounds fine." His scent drifted to her. Her lids fluttered.

"Let me know when you're ready."

Ready. There was that tone of invitation again, skidding up her spine.

"I could stay out here until sunrise," she said, wistfully gazing out to the horizon. "But —" she angled her head toward him "— I do have a busy day tomorrow."

Connor placed his hand at the dip in her back again. She sucked in air.

"Then, I'd better get you home."

"I really appreciate this," Olivia said while she fastened her seat belt. The entire interior of the vehicle held his scent, something hunky and sensual that she couldn't quite name but wanted more of.

"Not a problem. Besides —" he put the car in gear "— I was ready to leave. These gatherings aren't really my thing."

"I would have never thought that."

The corner of his mouth lifted in a half grin. "Why not?"

She recalled the way Lydia had clung to him, the way the women in the room reacted when he passed, his relaxed demeanor. "You seemed in your element. Comfortable."

"Looks can be deceiving," he said. "As we

both know from the work we do." He tossed her an amused look.

"Hmm, true," she conceded. "So why isn't it your thing?"

"Let's just say that the Lawson legacy is steeped in 'gatherings.' Instead of sleepovers or street games or sports with your friends, we were indoctrinated in the art of 'climbing the social ladder' through an endless stream of things like tonight."

The jaded tone of his voice was not lost on Olivia.

"I'd want to go hang out with my friends, drink, smoke, stuff that teens do, but I would be corralled along with my siblings and cousins to attend galas and coming-out parties and political fund-raisers." He pushed out a sigh. "So, yeah, I guess you could say that I appeared to be in my element. It's second nature. I can move through these things with my eyes closed." He turned his head toward her. "Then there you were."

A shiver raced through her system, halting her breath for a hot second. She didn't respond. She couldn't.

"And no . . . I don't say that to all the girls," he said, with a wink and a smile that loosened the knot in her throat.

"That's what all the boys say," she teased back.

"Touché."

They pulled onto the property of The Port.

"I'm on the end. At the top of the ridge."

Connor made the turn and continued on the short winding road.

"It's the one on the right."

He pulled up in front of her cottage and cut the engine.

Olivia's pulse kicked up a notch.

Connor opened his door and came around to open hers. He took her hand to help her to her feet. Only air separated them when she stood. She was forced to look up or stare at the three opened buttons of his black shirt. Staring into the dark depths of his eyes was worse. She felt as if she was falling until his arm snaked around her waist and he pulled her flush against him. Then the world disappeared. The hard lines of his body met her curves, and then he kissed her. Whatever sense she'd had of standing on solid ground was gone.

Olivia hungered after the pillow-soft yet firm feel of his luscious lips. The lingering sweet heat from his drink lingered on his mouth. Her tongue peeked out to take just a small taste, which set off a low rumble in his throat. His fingers pressed into the curve of her spine. Then, just as quickly as it had happened, it ended.

Connor took a step back, braced her waist with his hands. He tilted his head toward her front door. "You should go inside." His voice was so low, so deep and ragged that it reverberated inside her.

Olivia nodded. She stepped out of his light hold, walked around him and toward her front door. She took a look over her shoulder. "Thanks for the ride."

"Tuesday. Eight." He got back in his car, waited for her to step inside and then pulled off.

Olivia closed the door behind her, rested her back against the door and squeezed her eyes shut. She licked the taste of him off her bottom lip. "Connor Lawson. Damn, damn, damn."

CHAPTER 2

Olivia puttered around her cottage the following morning while reviewing her notes on the locations that she wanted to begin working on. One of them was just outside Azurest in a small enclave called Dayton Village. The schematics that she had of the landscape suggested it had been uninhabited for years. The few buildings that were left had been vacant for quite some time. According to the county clerk, the land still belonged to the descendants of the Dayton family, though none of them had lived in Sag Harbor for decades.

She packed up her laptop, her notes and camera and headed out, but decided to make a quick stop at the spa. Layla was Connor's cousin-in-law; perhaps she might have some insight into the intriguing Connor Lawson.

For the better part of her night Olivia had dreamed of him, felt his touch as clearly as if he was in the room with her. *And the kiss.* It still had her hot simply thinking of it and the way he'd made her feel.

However, Olivia didn't put much stake in anything long-term. If it wasn't related to her work, she didn't invest in anything that would involve her commitment. Long ago she'd had the rude awakening that feelings were only temporary — that relationships were only temporary, and to want more than that was foolish. So she'd built her emotional fortress, moved from place to place, relationship to relationship, job to job. Roots were things that she searched for, but never experienced in her own life. That was fine with her. She'd come to accept that this disconnect was her life. So as far as Connor Lawson was concerned, he was a hot, sexy man who could stir her pot, and when her project was over she would move on and so would he. That was just the way it was.

She put her laptop and camera in the trunk of her car, then drove the short distance from her cottage to the main building on the off chance that Layla had an opening in her schedule. When Olivia arrived, one of the first people that she ran into was Desiree, who was heading to the parking lot on her way into town.

"Hey, Olivia." She pulled her shades from her eyes. "You're up early."

"Wanted to get a jump on the day. And thanks again for inviting me to the party. I had a great time."

"Not a problem. Glad you could come. So —" she lifted a brow "— how did it go with Connor?" She gave her a cheeky grin.

Damn. The mere mention of his name did things to her. For an instant Olivia's thoughts scrambled, then settled. "Um, fine."

"Just fine?"

She adjusted her tote bag on her shoulder. "Well, we are getting together for drinks and dinner on Tuesday."

Desiree clapped her hands in delight. "Go 'head, girl. Women have been sniffing around that man from the instant he set foot in town and he has yet to give them anything more than that sexy smile and conversation."

Olivia's heart tumbled in her chest. "Really," she said casually.

"Yep. So you must have produced a spark. Anyway, I've got to run."

"Sure, go, go. I wanted to drop in at the spa and see if there were any openings for a quick massage."

Desiree gave her a knowing look. "Oh, you

mean with Connor's cousin Layla."

"They're cousins?" she asked with feigned surprise.

Desiree chuckled. "I'm sure Layla would be happy to tell you anything you wanted to know about her bachelor cousin, except that she and Maurice are in New York for the next two weeks working on Maurice's foundation for wounded soldiers. That's why they weren't at the party last night."

Olivia's shoulders drooped.

"But if you can't wait to find out on your own, Melanie Harte knows all. And she would love to think that once again she was involved in a *love* connection." Desiree grinned and patted Olivia's arm.

"Thanks. I think I'll wait."

"Good move. Anyway, gotta go. See you soon. Okay?"

"Sure thing. And thanks."

Desiree hurried away and Olivia returned to where she'd parked her car. So much for that brilliant idea. But it was just as well. She didn't want to come across as one of "those women" that did recon work on a man. That wasn't her style. Mostly, she had a short list of criteria for the attributes of the men she allowed in her life: good looks and intelligence, and not looking for or expecting a commitment. So far, Connor

Lawson fit the bill to a T, not to mention that they both had plenty in common from their chosen fields of work. She slid behind the wheel of her car and turned the key. In truth, what else did she need to know? Whatever might happen between them would last only as long as her assignment anyway. It was best that her knowledge remained superficial. The less you knew, the less you could be drawn into the life and wants and dreams and desires of someone else. She didn't need that, didn't want it and couldn't give it. She reserved those energies for her work and that was it.

Connor had been up before sunrise. Since moving to Sag Harbor he'd become addicted to rising before daybreak and running along the beach until the sun fully crested the horizon. The sensation of one man being that in tune with nature was indescribable. It gave him a rush that was close to orgasmic. It was his time. His alone time when he cleansed his head and his spirit.

But while he was running, for the first time, he wanted to share the experience with someone, and Olivia flashed in his head. He didn't know why, but he felt deep in his gut that she would appreciate the experience as much as he did, without him having to explain.

Most of the night he'd thought about Olivia, reimagined what she'd felt like when he'd touched her, what she'd tasted like when he'd kissed her. It wasn't often that a single encounter with an attractive woman kept him in a state of randy heat. It was ridiculous how many times he'd had to think of trucks instead of the hot spot between her legs. And if he didn't get his head in the game, he would waste an entire morning musing on "what if."

Today, he and his small crew were working on what had once been the main house in the small settlement. According to documents, the home was the first one built and was the largest, so that it could accommodate the new settlers until they were able to build places of their own.

Connor got out of his truck and trotted down the small incline to where the workers were gathered to talk about the day's assignment. Jake Thornton was his foreman and closest thing to a best friend. He was explaining to the crew what Connor wanted accomplished when Connor joined them.

"Morning, guys," Connor greeted the ten-man crew, and adjusted his sunglasses against the morning glare. "I know Jake got you all up to speed. We have a lot to achieve today. Forecast is for a late-afternoon storm. We need to work fast and efficiently." He turned to Jake. "How's the roof?"

"I have the roofers coming in about noon. I need them to do as much as they can as fast as they can. We can't afford water damage at this stage of the reno. Worst case is we'll use what tarp we have if the rains come before they get here."

Connor nodded. "Okay." He turned his intense focus on his team. "Let's get busy. We'll break for lunch at noon when the roofers arrive."

Connor and Jake broke away from the team and walked over to Jake's Ford truck. "How was that thing up on the hill last night?" Jake asked as he tapped a Newport cigarette from the pack and tucked it between his lips. He dug a lighter from his pocket and lit the end.

"You know how those things are. Lot of fancy." He chuckled. "Good food, great drinks, long legs." He laughed again and leaned back against the side of the truck. He crossed his arms. "Met this woman last night."

Jake gave a side glance, raised his chin and blew a puff of smoke into the air. "And . . ."

Connor searched around for words. "Nice.

She's an anthropologist working on a research project. Ancestry of the original families here."

Jake's brow lifted. "Hmm. Right up your alley."

Connor shrugged with indifference. "Just business. Two ships passing in the night, as the saying goes."

"Works for me." Jake dropped the butt of his cigarette on the ground and crushed it out with the heel of his construction boot.

"Taking her to dinner on Tuesday," Connor added, not quite ready to let the conversation wind down.

"Oh, now, that's news." His friend angled his long frame toward Connor. "She must be impressive if she got you to ask her to dinner."

"She's different." He still couldn't put his finger on what it was about Olivia that had him rethinking his usual game plan.

"Must be. The waiting line was long. I had my money on Lydia." Jake laughed.

Connor flashed him a look of total disbelief. "Lydia." He shook his head. "Not in a million years. Definitely not my type."

"Couldn't tell her that." Jake laughed again and pushed away from the truck. "I'll have to meet this Olivia," he said as they walked back toward the work site.

"Just two ships, man. Two ships."

"If you say so." He clapped Connor on the back.

To think that it could be more than temporary was a big mistake. It always was. Dina, Mya, Lynn, Sybil . . . The list was long and diverse. A different woman for a different city, a different job. It simply went with the territory. Then once they found out who he was, who his family was, the speed of "love" went from zero to one hundred in the blink of an eye.

He almost resented his family name and legacy at times, which only fueled the bad blood between him and his father. So rather than fight what had become the inevitable spiral of his relationships, he kept them brief and emotion-free. Many women thought it was arrogance or privilege that wafted around him like a protective shield. In truth it was self-preservation. When he decided that he was ready to open himself up to the possibility of something real, the woman had to be damned spectacular.

Then along had come Adrienne . . . He shook the memory away. His thoughts drifted to Olivia Gray.

"What are you grinning about?"

Connor blinked and Jake came into focus. He clapped Jake on the back. "Nothing, man. Let's get to work."

Connor soon became immersed in his work and the images and stirring thoughts of Olivia drifted into the backdrop of his day. The team had been working steadily, hauling away debris and shoring up weak foundations, when the roofers finally arrived.

"And not a minute too soon," Jake said, glancing skyward.

Overstuffed clouds lumbered along the skyline and shifted their appearance from dull white to dove gray. Beyond the crest of the horizon a line of ominous darkness pushed across the water and above the trees.

"Tell the guys to pack it up. Let the roofers do their thing. I'll stay and make sure that we don't get a washout," Connor said.

"My sentiments exactly." Jake turned to go round up the men.

Connor rolled up the blueprints, but his attention was drawn toward the sound of another car coming their way. He lifted his work goggles from his eyes. The auto summiting the rise came into view. He'd expected that it would be the roofers, but clearly, the Range Rover was not carrying the crew.

The car came to a stop and the driver shut the engine.

"Probably another tourist," Jake said. "I'll get rid of them." He started toward the car. Connor stopped him with a firm grip on his forearm.

Olivia stepped out of the car and gazed around before spotting Connor.

"You go ahead. I'll take care of it." He shoved his goggles into his shirt pocket, took off his work gloves and began walking toward Olivia.

As he drew closer he realized that his pulse was racing. He was in excellent physical shape and the short walk up the incline should have had no bearing on his heart rate.

"Hey," he said, stopping in front of her. "What are you doing here?"

"Hi. We were so busy talking around our current projects I never made the connection that we could possibly be working on the same job."

Connor frowned in bemusement. "Same job?" He angled his head to the side.

Olivia dug in her carryall and pulled out a sheaf of documents. "Unless there's another Dayton Village, I'm in the right place." She flipped through a couple pages and then showed him the paperwork detailing her assignment.

"You're definitely in the right place." He

handed her back the documents. “I’m just the lowly rehab guy. Why would anyone bother to tell me? *You’re* the doc.”

Olivia inwardly flinched at the jab. “What’s that supposed to mean?”

He flipped her a half grin. “Nothing at all. We were getting ready to wrap up. Storm’s coming.”

Olivia glanced skyward as if she had to confirm what he said for herself.

“Hey, boss,” Jake said, coming up alongside Connor. “We’re done. The roofers can take it from here.” He eyed Olivia.

“Thanks.” He lifted his chin in her direction. “Jake, this is Dr. Olivia Gray.”

Jake’s eyes momentarily widened, but he held his tongue. He extended his hand. “Nice to meet you, Dr. Gray.”

“You, too,” she murmured.

“We’ll be seeing much more of Dr. Gray. Apparently she’s been assigned to research the site.” He shoved his hands into his pants pockets.

A bang of thunder boomed in the heavens, punctuating Connor’s comment.

“Oh. Well, if you have any questions . . .” Jake let the comment hang in the charged air. “I’m going to head out, boss. See you in the a.m.”

“Yeah. Tomorrow.”

Jake walked away and headed for his car.

The sky grew ominously dark.

Connor faced Olivia just as the first plop of rain fell. "I'm going to wait for the roofers to finish," he said dismissively.

"You want to tell me what bug got up your ass?" she retorted.

Connor was so stunned that he almost laughed. He never would have thought that Olivia Gray would drop the lady decorum and show this side of herself. She had a spicy tongue. Although he really shouldn't be surprised. He'd felt it last night. Tasted it. Behind the cultured talk and proper attitude was a woman on simmer, right below the surface. The instant he'd kissed her, he'd known.

Connor flexed his hard jaw. "Bug up my ass? Hmm." He snorted a laugh. "Let's say that I don't like surprises and you . . . were a surprise." The last woman who'd been on one of his reno sites had tried to turn his project into her own personal HGTV reality show when she'd shown up on-site with a camera crew. He'd nearly lost his own crew in that fiasco, along with his credibility — since he'd been sleeping with her.

Olivia drew in a breath and slowly exhaled. "I'm as surprised as you are. I had no idea this was the rehab project you were working on." Her eyes cinched at the corner. "Do you think I was trying to undermine you in some way . . . because of last night? Some kind of dumb setup?"

She'd read him like an open book. "The thought briefly ran through my head."

"You have got to be kidding," she said, enunciating every word.

His right brow flicked but he didn't respond.

"Let's get one thing straight, Mr. Lawson. I'm a professional. I don't need to wheedle my way into any situation to get what I want. And I certainly don't need the all clear from you to do my job."

The rain had gone from a plop to a sprinkle.

He held his hands up, palms facing her. "If you say so."

Her shoulders tightened, as did her expression.

"There aren't many people that I run into that don't want something. There's always some agenda." His dark, haunted eyes moved by degrees across her face.

"Every now and then, Mr. Lawson," she said softly, "there's an exception to your rule."

The rain came down harder.

He shifted his weight to relieve the sudden throb in his pants. “I have to wait for the roofers to finish,” he repeated, as if the statement would send her on her way.

Thunder rumbled like the stomach of a starving man.

“Do you mind if I wait with you? I’d like to take a look around.” She wiped water from her face.

He knew damned good and well that was a very bad idea. But what the hell. If they had to work together they may as well be cordial. “Sure. Come on before we really get drenched.” He took her arm and hustled her down the ridge to the main building. “And maybe you can call me Connor again,” he shouted over the roll of thunder.

“We’ll see, Mr. Lawson,” she teased, as they ran like children chased by the bolts of lightning that lit up the early-afternoon sky.

Connor chuckled to himself as he pushed open the door. She would. If he wasn’t sure about anything else today, he was sure of that.

The interior was dark, more so because of the lack of sunlight. Olivia shook off the water while Connor turned on the generator that lit the lights.

“No place like home,” he joked as dirt and dust swirled in the air and settled.

Olivia wiped water from her face and

looked around. Immediately she was thrown back in time. She could feel the spirits of the ancestors who had found their new lives and freedom within these walls. The energy was palpable. She wrapped her arms around her body and slowly walked around, taking in as much as she could in the muted light. She ran her hand along the scarred oak mantel of the hearth, the frames of the makeshift windows, the warped wood of the walls.

Connor closely watched the awe move in slow waves across Olivia's face, the wonder in her eyes. He knew what she was feeling. He'd been there, felt it whenever he worked on a project like this.

She spun toward him. "This place is amazing." Her eyes were wide as she lifted her gaze to the rafters of the cabin. "The write-ups and diagrams do it no justice. I can't wait to get started. How many buildings have you worked on so far?"

"We've done mostly shoring-up work. The structures are pretty worn and weak from water damage, rot and age. Before we can do any restoration we have to make sure the structures are stable."

"Of course," she said in a faraway voice, while she continued to explore. "There's so much history here that's not visible to the naked eye."

Connor leaned casually against the wall. He folded his arms. "What had you planned on doing first?"

Olivia focused on him. She exhaled slowly. "I'd like to examine anything that has been left behind — chairs, boxes, cabinets, bedding, old clothing, photos, papers, draperies, all the artifacts. Pretty much any and everything beyond the actual structures. What I want to do is to begin to build a picture, piece together the story of this community and try to match it up with any written documentation."

Connor grinned. "My job is *so* much easier than yours."

She returned his smile. "This is the fun part — the hunt, the discovery." She walked to the far side of the room. "Mind if I take some pictures?" She already had her camera out before he had a chance to respond.

"What if I'd said no?"

Olivia peeked at him from above the camera lens and clicked. "And why would you do that?" she teased in a singsong voice.

Connor chuckled to himself. This woman was the real thing. She may have been taking pictures, but so was he. He studied her; visually strolled along the dips and curves of her lithe body, memorized the way the dim light lit a honey-tinged fire in her eyes. The energy that wafted from her was an aphrodisiac that whetted his hunger. He shifted his body weight and shoved his hands into his pockets. She bent down to get a snapshot and he took a picture of her luscious rear end. Deep in his chest he hummed in appreciation, and clenched his jaw to keep from groaning out loud. What he wanted to do was snatch her up in his arms and take her breath away with a real kiss, not like the preliminary one of last night.

The sudden blare of a honking horn brought them both up short.

"Must be my roofers needing something. Be right back." He brushed by her on the way out and caught a whiff of scent that nearly stopped him in his tracks. He pulled open the door and stepped out into a steady rainfall.

Once he was gone, Olivia dared to breathe. Her heart pounded and her fingers trembled. She leaned against the wall and momentarily closed her eyes. If there was the slightest thought in her head that working side by side with Connor Lawson was going to be easy, she was dead wrong. Her thoughts were in a jumble when he was in her airspace. It was a wonder she uttered anything that made sense. Crazy. This was so unlike her. But there was something about Connor from the moment she'd laid eyes on him that had unsettled her way down to the essence of her being. Clearly she couldn't do her job if she didn't get her head in the game. Maybe she should just go to bed with him and get it out of her system. *Both* of their systems — because she knew he felt the same way.

She ran her fingers through her damp hair. Yes, that was what she'd do. Screw his brains out and then *she* could think clearly.

The door pushed open. Connor stood in the doorway with the darkened sky as his backdrop, and the raw, animal energy that pushed out of his pores was palpable. His shirt was soaked and clung to the hard outline of his chest, the concave slope of his belly. She wouldn't look any farther. She didn't dare.

Connor wiped water from his face. "It's getting pretty messy out there. I need to hang around until they're done with the emergency work. You should probably head on out."

To Olivia's ears he didn't sound very convincing about why she should leave. Her heart thumped and thumped. "Um, how long do you think they'll be?"

"An hour, maybe less. They're working fast. Fortunately they got started just before it really started coming down. Now it's a matter of securing what they've put up."

"I'm not really in a hurry." She gave a slight shrug of her left shoulder.

He hesitated for a moment, weighed the options. "I guess I could show you some of the other structures if you don't mind getting wet."

"Not at all."

"Come on. I'll show you where the property begins . . . at least where we think it does." He walked to the door and held it open.

Olivia gathered her things, stuck her camera back in her bag and walked toward him. She stopped in the doorway and was reminded once again of the pure virility of the man when the top of her head brushed beneath his chin and her shoulder came in contact with the rock hard chest. Tremors skittered along her spine and made the hairs on the back of her neck stand up.

Connor snatched up an umbrella that was leaning against the wall, stepped out and popped it open. "Don't want you to get too wet."

Olivia licked away the retort with a swipe

of her tongue. She was already wet in ways that he could only imagine. "Thanks," she said instead, and ducked under the offered shelter, closing the space between them.

Connor guided her along the roughed-out path that led to a row of what could barely be called buildings. They were the equivalent of children's drawings, sitting at odd angles due to years of the makeshift foundations sinking into the ground. Doors were askew or missing altogether. Some structures reminded her of Halloween jack-o-lanterns, with dark cutouts for the missing windows and gouged-out ragged steps that appeared to laugh at the observers. But Olivia knew that the exterior was only the pathway to hidden treasures beyond the weather-beaten walls.

They stopped at the roofers' truck.

"We should be done in about another twenty minutes or so, Mr. Lawson," the foreman said. "Your men did a good job of getting the temporary tarp up. We're finishing with the sealing and checking for leaks. When you're ready we'll be back for something more permanent."

"Thanks, Bobby. Oh, this is Dr. Olivia Gray. She's doing some research so you may run into her again."

Bobby tugged off his glove and stuck out

his hand. "Pleasure. What kind of doctor?"

"Anthropologist."

A cloud of confusion moved across his face, which was crisscrossed with lines from years of working under the beating sun. "Sounds important."

Olivia smiled. "Nice to meet you."

Connor cupped Olivia's elbow and guided her toward another of the buildings.

"Watch yourself coming up the steps," he warned. He extended his hand to help her and sent a jolt of something tingly racing up her arm when his fingers wrapped around hers.

Olivia sidestepped a gaping hole and hopped up the last step. Connor opened the door.

The interior was dim, the barest hint of light inching through a sliver of space between the slatted wood walls. The odd shapes of old furnishings draped in sheets and dust cast cartoonish images on the walls and hard-packed dirt floor.

Connor flipped a switch and the portable floodlight pushed soft white light into the space, throwing every object into sharp relief.

Olivia's eyes adjusted and she was instantly taken back hundreds of years. In the corner, the old wood-burning stove still held the huge cast-iron pot waiting to be filled. Spectral images moved around the square room, carrying wood, sweeping the floors, laughing, kissing, arguing. Children played and babies cried.

Olivia jumped when Connor touched her arm. She blinked and it was only the two of them.

"You okay?"

She swallowed and focused on his expression of concern, the way his sleek dark brows drew close. That was when she realized that her heart was racing. "Yes. Fine. This all feels a bit surreal."

He pushed out a breath. "I know exactly what you mean. I felt the same way the first time I came into this room. I felt a presence, a warmth."

"Exactly!" She wouldn't tell him that she swore she'd seen images of the former inhabitants. She didn't want him to think that she was crazy. *She* didn't want to think that *she* was crazy. "It's all so amazing." She walked around the space, ran her hand along the knobby wood, stooped down to get a better look at the stone hearth.

Connor stepped back into the shadows of the room to better watch her movements. He leaned against the wall, studied the precision and economy of everything that she did and wondered what she would be like under his touch. Would she forego her efficiency and take her time, let him take his time? He didn't want her perfect. He wanted her raw and real, no holds barred.

The sound of clicking and soft flashes of light snapped him to attention.

"Hope you don't mind," Olivia said, as she moved fluidly around the space, snapping photos. "Couldn't resist." She swung around in his direction and took three pictures in rapid succession. She lowered the camera and smiled at him. "Now you're a part of history."

Connor chuckled. He took a step toward her. The shout of his name, along with the sound of knocking, stopped him. His jaw reflexively tightened. He turned to the door and pulled it open.

The roofer stepped in out of the rain. "All done, Mr. Lawson." He wiped the water from his face. "Sealed everything. It should hold you until we can get in and do the real work that's needed."

"Good." Connor nodded his head. "Thanks for coming out on such short notice, Bobby." He stuck out his hand, enclosing the smaller hand of the roofer in a firm grip.

"Anytime."

"Let's take a quick look at what got done before your crew heads out."

"Sure thing, Mr. Lawson." He stepped back outside.

Connor turned toward Olivia. "Ready?"

"Sure." She put her camera back in her tote and hoisted it onto her right shoulder.

Connor took the umbrella from the corner and handed it to Olivia. He turned off the floodlight and everything was momentarily reduced to memory. Connor pushed open the door and she saw his silhouette return, flush against the dull gray afternoon.

Olivia opened the umbrella and gingerly inched around the hole in the step and down onto solid ground. Connor followed, then ducked beneath the umbrella, reflexively scooping his arm around her waist. It was intimate, cocooned together, shielded from the elements and separated from the world around them.

She forced herself to concentrate on not tumbling into some unseen ditch, rather than the heat and soap-and-water scent of Connor's body, which was barely a breath away from hers.

"What's on your agenda for the rest of the day?" Connor asked as he gently guided her down the short incline toward her parked car.

Olivia cleared her throat. "I have some research to do. I need to review all of my notes and start mapping out a workable schedule."

"When will you be back?"

"I'm hoping as soon as tomorrow." It was part question, part statement. She quickly glanced at his rugged profile, his jaw outlined in a well-trimmed five-o'clock shadow.

They stopped in front of her vehicle.

He faced her. "Hopefully we won't get in each other's way." His gaze held her fixed to the spot.

Olivia held her breath, certain that he was going to kiss her. She wanted him to.

Thunder slowly rolled across the heavens.

Connor reached around her and opened the door. "Give me a call when you're on your way."

A wave of disappointment swam through her. She blinked it away and smiled. "Sure." She slid in behind the wheel. Her eyes rolled up to him and suddenly everything disappeared as he leaned down and covered her mouth with his. Only for an instant, but long enough to reawaken the taste of him, heat her in the center of her belly. Then it was over, but her heart still raced.

"Drive safely." He stroked her cheek with the barest tip of his finger. "Talk to you tomorrow."

Olivia swallowed and ran her tongue along her bottom lip. All she could do was nod her head in agreement.

Connor shut her door and stepped back.

Olivia fumbled with the key, finally got it in the ignition and turned on the car. When she looked out her window, Connor was halfway across the grounds and soon disappeared behind one of the buildings.

CHAPTER 3

Connor returned to the makeshift office, took off his wet jacket and hung it on a hook behind the door. For a moment he shut his eyes and drew in a long, deep breath. He shouldn't have let her go. He should have invited her to . . . something, whatever it took to keep her with him a bit longer.

He shook his head. Crazy. Losing his grip over some woman that he barely knew? What was that about? His cell phone vibrated in his pocket. He pulled it out. It was a call from Jake.

"Hey, Jake. What's up?"

"Just checking. The roofers done?"

"Yeah, they left a little while ago. Everything looks good. We should be okay."

"Great. Listen, me and some of the fellas are in town catching a few beers and the game."

Connor didn't make it a habit of hanging out with his crew. It wasn't that he didn't enjoy their company. It was more that he was mindful of crossing the line from employer to friend. But today he didn't feel like being in his own company. To do that would keep him under the spell of whatever it was that Olivia Gray had cast over him. Maybe a roomful of male testosterone fueled by beer guzzling and cussing, and further incited by the sight of bodies crashing into each other on the field, was what he needed.

"Yeah, yeah, I think I will. Everyone at McCoy's?"

"Back room."

Connor chuckled. "A regular party. See you in a few." He disconnected the call and was actually looking forward to some male bonding.

By the time Connor arrived at McCoy's the weather had somewhat cleared. At least the rain had stopped, but it left behind a misty residue that hung waiflike above the town. Connor found a parking spot in the lot behind the bar, then joined the crew inside.

The back room of McCoy's was about the size of a small classroom. A fifty-inch television was mounted on the paneled wall, wooden circular tables with spindle-backed chairs dotted the plank-wood floor and in the far corner was a jukebox with nothing more current than hits from the eighties.

McCoy's prided itself on the bare essentials of its establishment. What it lacked in ambience it made up for with some of the best wings, ribs, steaks and burgers this side of the Mississippi, and drinks that could lay you on your ass, not like the watered-down stuff at some of the higher-end restaurants. McCoy's was a sports pub through and through.

"Connor, over here." Jake stood and waved him over to a back table.

Connor acknowledged the faces he knew with a lift of his chin as he passed by. The room was in full swing and the one waitress that was assigned to the space had her hands full keeping up with the orders. He made his way around the tables and pulled up a chair.

"First things first," Connor said as he sat down. "What's the score and how long will it take to get a drink?"

The table of five laughed heartily and brought Connor up to speed on the game. They were split down the middle between the Giants and the Redskins. There was money and booze on the table. It could go either way. Connor tossed his hat in with the Giants, ordered a bourbon neat and a burger with all the trimmings.

Jake scooted his chair a bit closer. "So how'd it go?" he asked, loud enough for Connor to hear but not their tablemates.

Connor glanced at him over the rim of his glass. "Told you. Fine. We're good to go for tomorrow."

"You know I wasn't talking about the roofers." His right brow arched.

Connor chuckled. "That went fine, too, or as fine as it could go under the circumstances."

"To tell you the truth, I kinda thought the two of you would have been together right about now. Although I was hoping not, at least not until her agenda is clear," he added, with a look that spoke to the last woman on the site. "Didn't expect you to accept the invite."

Connor took a sip of his bourbon, let it slowly warm his insides. "You were almost right." He stared off into the distance. A glimmer of a smile teased the corners of his mouth. "We'll see," he said, and tossed back the rest of his drink while dismissing the subject of Olivia Gray.

Olivia pulled the belt on her robe a bit tighter, turned off the flame beneath the pot of boiling water, then poured it over her chamomile tea bag. She took her cup to the table where she'd spread out her notes. Settling in, she slowly glanced over the pages of documents and the sketches of what was once Dayton Village. She powered on her MacBook and scrolled to the images she'd uploaded earlier. It was still very early in the process but she could barely contain the excitement that bubbled in her veins. There was something different about this, a feeling she had that whatever she uncovered would change her in some way. It was a ridiculous notion, of course, but she couldn't shake it. She'd done dozens and dozens of these investigative projects, and yes, there was always a level of excitement — anticipation . . . but . . .

The picture that she'd shot of Connor leaning against the wall came to life on her computer screen, and her heart jumped in response. There was no doubt that Connor Lawson added another dimension to the work. The idea of working with him over the days and weeks to come felt like sitting at the top of a roller coaster waiting for the crazy thrill ride. Seeing Connor forever captured on film stirred the embers of that first night, when he'd taken her home, kissed her, left her wanting more.

Olivia closed her eyes against the taunt of

his hard outline and returned her attention to her notes. One of the first things that she needed to do was photograph the entire site. She would compare those images to the diagrams and then begin her interviews and study the artifacts on the site. Often the tiniest remain would hold a wealth of information. Her pulse quickened at the thought of the treasures that she was sure to uncover. Having Connor Lawson in her peripheral vision was a bonus.

She sipped her tea and flipped through her binder. She stopped on the articles that documented the first family of Dayton Village. According to historical documents, Elijah and Sarah Dayton arrived from Virginia at the turn of the century. Both Elijah and Sarah were born into slavery, a year before the Emancipation. Based on the minimal information at Olivia's disposal, the couple had several children, all of whom they raised in Dayton Village. Not much more was known about them. At some point others found their way to the village and built new lives there.

Olivia's thoughts wandered, envisioning the time, the early days when Dayton Village first began, the excitement and uncertainty that must have permeated everything and everyone. She could almost feel the hope of the people who'd come there so many years ago wanting to build a life on the shoulders of freedom. She could only imagine what it must have been like for the thousands of Africans torn from their homeland, doomed to a life of slavery and degradation, to one day be free. It meant different things to so many people. As the legendary conductor Harriet Tubman once said, "I freed hundreds of slaves and could have freed hundreds more if they knew they were slaves."

That very powerful statement resonated within Olivia like none other. How can people know where they can go, what they can achieve and the possibilities that await, if they don't know who they are in the world — what was their purpose?

It was not happenstance that of all the professions to choose from, Olivia decided to study anthropology. She was led in that direction because her own life was riddled with missing pieces, inconsistencies and half-truths. If she couldn't construct the foundation of her own truth, then she would do it for others.

Her cell phone vibrated on the countertop. She smiled at the Bach ring tone that was attributed to Dr. Victor Randall, her supervisor and on again, off again lover.

Olivia pressed the green phone icon. “Victor, checking up on me?” She leaned against the backrest of the chair.

“Yes.” He chuckled. “How are things — and you, of course?”

“Well, I had a chance to briefly visit the site yesterday, but the weather was against us. I did get some photographs and . . . I met with the developer in charge of the restoration work.”

“Connor Lawson.”

Olivia beat back the sudden uptick of her heart. She drew in a breath. “Uh, yes, as a matter of fact.”

“Hmm. Heard good things about his work. It’s really important that you two work hand in hand. Not only do we want to get the history of Dayton Village, but it’s going to be up to you to ensure that the restoration keeps in line with your findings.”

Olivia frowned. “Mr. Lawson doesn’t seem to be the kind of man that would appreciate outside direction on his project.”

“I’m not telling you to run his project. What I’m saying is that it’s imperative for our purposes to ensure that the restoration remains true to your findings. The site . . . is the only original community of freed slaves and Native American Indians on the Eastern Seaboard. I can’t impress upon you the significance of that. You are the eyes and ears. You are the one who must ensure that every detail is accurate."

"I've been doing this for a long time, long enough to appreciate the significance without a reminder course." She felt his hesitation before he responded.

"I didn't mean to imply otherwise or to second-guess you. However, the grant is important, Liv. Plenty of eyes are watching. If we miss a step on this project we could potentially lose major funding across the board for the future. Not to mention that your five-year contract is up at the end of this project. I don't have to tell you what that means."

Olivia blew out a conciliatory breath. "I know." The weight of her responsibility and her future curved her shoulders.

"I plan to come down in a couple of weeks," Victor said.

Olivia flinched. "Why? I mean, sure, but . . . why?"

"The funders want a progress report and . . . I want to see you."

Her stomach knitted. She looped her fingers around her mug, as she'd suddenly grown inexplicably cold. She brought the mug to her lips and took a sip. "Looking forward," she finally said.

“I’ll only be able to stay a couple of days . . . but I hope we can spend some time together, catch up. It’s been too long.”

A filmstrip of their relationship played in front of her. Dr. Victor Randall could have easily had any woman that he wanted. He was a brilliant scientist with magazine looks, and a personality that was a mixture of charm and sensuality. They’d met about four years earlier when Olivia had first come to work at The Institute. He became her mentor, then her lover, then her supervisor. They’d both agreed that neither of them wanted or needed anything permanent. When Victor got his promotion, they’d tempered their personal relationship, and over time their intimacy moved further into the background, morphing into what it was today — purely platonic as far as Olivia was concerned. Even though she’d made it crystal clear that nothing could happen between them, there were instances when Victor seemed to have forgotten.

“It has,” she finally responded, her voice noncommittal. “Um, just let me know when.”

“I will.” He paused. “Is everything all right, Liv? You sound . . . odd.”

She pushed away thoughts of Connor and Victor in the same space, with her in the middle. "No. I'm fine. Looking over some notes and thinking about your visit." She heard him exhale.

"Good. I'll be in touch soon."

"Take care, Victor." She disconnected the call and slowly placed the phone on the counter. She stared off across the kitchen. Maybe having Victor come for a visit was a necessary complication. Connor Lawson would only wind up being "another one," and she wasn't sure if that was all she wanted. Victor's presence would erect the barrier she needed to prevent that from happening.

Olivia turned off her computer and stuck her loose pages back into the binders. It was nearly ten. She was sure that the workers at the site would be in full swing by now. She would need access, but she didn't want to get in the way. Unfortunately, she and Connor hadn't discussed a working schedule. She hopped down from the chair. There was no time like the present.

After getting dressed in her typical workday outfit of jeans, white cotton blouse and ankle boots, she gathered her iPad, notebook, phone and camera and tossed them in her tote. She grabbed her lightweight leather jacket from the hook by the door and headed out.

Unlike the previous day, the forecast was for warm weather and blue skies. Signs of spring were everywhere, on the budding leaves and shimmering grass. The chirps of the winged ones that had begun to return from a winter hiatus carried the announcement of a new beginning.

Olivia rolled down her window and inhaled the freshly washed air; the sharp scents of wet grass and moist earth permeated her senses. On either side of the narrow two-lane road the small, neat homes stood like advertisements for a way of life that was foreign to city living.

Moments like these, and of course, the thrill of discovery, were the ingredients that fueled her, made all the traveling and often long, grueling hours worthwhile. Uncovering the history of people long forgotten and bringing them back to life for the world to see was an unending goal. It was all she had; it was who she was. There was a time in her life when that stark reality had stared her in the face and she'd been overcome by an unbearable sense of worthlessness. Over time, rather than reject or fight the one fact of her life that she could believe in, she'd embraced it.

Yet there were moments like now, as the

homestead came into view, and she knew the buried secrets of some others' past would soon be revealed, that she wanted more for herself for once.

Olivia cut the engine of the Range Rover, gathered her things and got out. She stood for a moment on the crest overlooking the worn structures and forgotten paths below. She pulled out her camera and took a series of shots of the work in progress to document the "before." She put her camera away and cupped her hands around her eyes, blocking out the glare of the morning sun in hopes of spotting Connor among the men. Her heart double-timed with anticipation as she slowly descended the slope and made her way across the muddy ground and around the trucks and heavy equipment.

A tingle skittered along her spine. His voice. She heard him before she saw him. She turned to her right and caught sight of him climbing up onto the seat of a tractor. Halfway in he stopped, as if he'd heard something in the distance that told him to wait. Hanging on to the wheel, he swiveled his hard body in Olivia's direction.

The only thing that moved was her lips, which parted ever so slightly to gather some air.

Connor jumped down, snatched his thick

work gloves off his hands and jammed them into his back jeans' pocket while he strode toward her.

Olivia clenched her fist, digging her nails into her palm. The mildly uncomfortable action snapped her back to the reality of where she was and why. She was not here to snatch this fine specimen of a man by his leather belt and haul him into one of these deserted buildings. That was not her assignment.

"Olivia," he said in greeting, making her name sound like a hymn.

"I should have called or something, but I did want to get started. Maybe we can work out some kind of schedule." She wished that she could see his eyes behind his dark shades.

The left corner of his lush mouth inched slightly upward. "It's not a problem. Really. You can come . . . whenever you want."

Her clit jumped at the double entendre.

"We can work out a schedule tomorrow night — at dinner."

Her eyes widened for a fraction of a second, but it wasn't lost on Connor.

"We're still on . . . ?"

"Yes. Sure. I'm looking forward to it," Connor said.

He studied her for a moment from behind

the shield of darkness. "So . . . where do you want to start?"

"Well, I thought I'd begin by matching up the drawings with the structures that are standing — do some sketches. Then, going forward, examining each of the buildings, the areas around them, checking for artifacts, note taking, more pictures." She grinned. "Ideally, I need to get in before any major restoration is done. I'd also want to examine any debris."

"Whatever you need." He cleared his throat. "I'll get Jake to take you around."

Why was she disappointed? She forced a smile. "Great."

"He's on the other side. Follow me."

Connor walked a step or two ahead of Olivia and she cataloged the confident, long-legged swagger that could part a crowd or the seven seas. She drew in a "get it together" breath and matched his pace.

"What time do you want me to pick you up?"

"Oh, um, seven, seven thirty." She glanced at his profile.

Connor gave a bare nod, then lifted his chin. "Over this way."

Jake was in the midst of reviewing the blueprints with one of the crew when Olivia and Connor walked up.

"Connor. Dr. Gray." His greeting held a questioning note. He glanced from one to the other.

"Dr. Gray wants to get started with her research. We'll work out some kind of schedule, but I told her that you'd give her the full tour in the meantime."

A brief shadow of confusion passed over Jake's face. He gave a slight shrug. "Sure." He flashed a look at Connor, but couldn't penetrate the dark lenses.

"When you're done, come back to the main building," Connor said, and strode off.

Olivia watched him leave and juggled the conflicting emotions that followed — dismissal, disappointment, uncertainty.

"Ready?"

Olivia blinked and turned her focus on Jake. "Yes." She adjusted her tote on her shoulder and fell into step with him. "I hope this isn't too much of an inconvenience."

"Not at all. What the boss wants the boss gets. We can start up on the ridge and work our way down and across," he quickly added, before Olivia could respond to the "boss" comment.

"Lead the way."

"You do a lot of these, I suppose," Jake said.

Olivia smiled. “I’ve had my share. You?”

“Working with Connor is a lot different from what I’d been doing.”

“What was that?”

“Basic construction work, apartments and office buildings mostly.”

“So . . . how did you and Connor meet?”

Jake slowed in front of a structure that was standing with a hope and a prayer. “Funny, seems as if I’ve known him all my life.” His brow knit. “We were at this bar in Harlem, Rhythms I think was the name. We had a few drinks, started talking and the next thing I knew I was saying yes to joining him on his next reno job. One job led to the next.” He shrugged. “Here we are.”

“He must be a very persuasive guy.”

Jake gave her a sidelong glance from midnight-blue eyes. “Very. Connor always finds a way to get what he wants.” He picked up a yellow hard hat that was stored on the outside of the building and handed it to Olivia. “Can’t be too careful.” He unhooked his own from his work belt and put it on his head. He held open the door of the cabin and Olivia stepped inside.

For the next two hours, Jake led her around the development, explaining the layout and functions of each of the structures and what, if any, work had been done, while Olivia photographed and took notes. In between she asked innocuous questions about Connor, which Jake seemed more than happy to answer.

"See everything you need?" Connor asked when Olivia and Jake approached. He wiped his moist forehead with the back of his hand. At some point he'd taken off his gray hoodie and was now wearing only a fitted gray T-shirt that was sticking to his damp torso.

Olivia licked her bottom lip and tore her gaze away from the expanse of his chest, but looking into his now exposed eyes was just as deadly. "Jake was extremely helpful." She turned and flashed Jake a smile.

"Anytime. I'm gonna head back up the hill. The supplies came in. Need to check the inventory."

"Sure. And thanks." Connor focused on Olivia. He leaned against a mud-covered truck, crossed his feet at the ankle and stared at her, his gaze gently probing.

Olivia felt as if she was being caressed, but Connor was several feet away. Her skin tingled. She ran her hands up and down her arms.

"Cold?"

She shook her head. "Um, I'm going back to my place. I have a lot of work to do. Thanks for today."

"I'll walk you to your car." He stepped up to her, then casually placed his hand at the dip of her back, as if it was something he was entitled to do, and the warmth of his hand and his self-assurance flowed through her.

Olivia allowed herself to be guided around the workmen and their big toys. When she and Connor reached her Range Rover, she faced him. "How many more hours?" she asked, lifting her chin toward the work site.

"Till about six." He took a step. "I'd be in the mood for a drink about six thirty. Care to join me?" It sounded like a challenge.

"I . . . really have a lot to do . . ."

"No problem. If you change your mind, I'll be at McCoy's on Winston Street." He tapped the side of her car and walked away before she had a chance to respond.

Olivia tugged the door open and got behind the wheel. She should have agreed. Instead, she pulled away and went home . . . to spend the evening alone.

Chapter 4

"So . . . what do you think of Connor Lawson?" Desiree asked. She stuck her fork in the chicken salad and took a mouthful.

Olivia took a sip of her tea. "He's . . . nice enough."

Desiree nearly choked. "Nice enough. You. Are. Kidding. Right?"

Olivia laughed. "What do you want me to say, Desi?"

"I saw the two of you together at the party. There was definitely chemistry."

"I think you're imagining things."

"Hmm. And my name is Don't Know Any Better."

Olivia pushed out a feigned sigh. "Okay, okay, you twisted my arm. The man is fine. All caps. Sexy seeps from his pores *and* he's smart. Lethal combination. Would I kick him out of my bed? I don't think so," she added with a grin. "We're going to dinner tonight. So . . . we'll see." She gave a half shrug.

"That's more like it. Where are you going?"

"I have no idea." She picked up her chicken panino. "He didn't say, just that he was going to pick me up between seven and seven thirty."

Desiree leaned in. "Connor doesn't date."

"What?" Olivia frowned in confusion.

Desiree tilted her head to the side. "Connor is . . . How can I say this . . ."

"Just say it."

Desiree pursed her lips a moment before responding. "He's noncommittal. He may meet a woman at a party or a restaurant, but he doesn't do the 'date' thing. At least not in all the time he's been here." Her brows rose for emphasis.

"So . . . what are you telling me . . . exactly?"

"I'm saying that I think he likes you."

Olivia playfully rolled her eyes. "You're reading waaay too much into a simple dinner."

"Fine. But don't say I didn't warn you."

After lunch at The Port with Desiree, Olivia treated herself to a mani-pedi, followed by a stop at the local boutique. The bulk of her wardrobe was jeans, T-shirts and one dress fit for a corporate meeting, not a date with the hottest guy in town. But since she had no idea where they were going or what was de rigueur, she opted for the can't-go-wrong simple black dress with a cap sleeve, V-neckline that offered a hint of the gems beneath, and the hem just above her knees. The fabric was simple jersey that subtly cupped her curves. Her one pair of black dress shoes with a modest two-inch heel would do fine.

Olivia turned from side to side in front of the mirror and was pleased with her reflection, although she often wondered if she resembled anyone. Did she have her mother's wide doe-shaped eyes or her father's narrow nose? Whose genes had given her the tiny cleft in her chin? Was her nut-brown complexion a family trait? Did wild springy curls run in the family? As much as she wanted to stop asking the litany of questions, she never could. The answers were always out of her reach. She leaned forward and added a bit of bronze-toned lip gloss, then gave her naturally long lashes a couple of swipes of mascara.

Her cell phone shimmied across the dresser top. She snatched it up and pressed the green phone icon.

"Hello."

"Hey. I should be to you in about ten minutes. Ready?"

"Just about. See you then."

Olivia set the phone down and noticed that her hand was shaking every so slightly, as a warm flush, the kind you feel from good liquor, moved through her. She inhaled deeply, took her phone and keys from the dresser and dropped them both in her purse, smoothed her dress and then walked up front. For a few moments she practiced walking back and forth across the living room floor of her cottage rental. Walking and balancing in heels was a far cry from her sneakers and work shoes.

When she first arrived in Sag Harbor, she'd stayed at one of the hotels in town that overlooked Long Island Sound. She'd tried to get a place at The Port but was told they were booked solid. Where she wound up staying was nice enough as hotels go and she would have been content to stay, until she'd run into Desiree Davenport one day at the local vegetable market. They'd hit it off right away and Olivia had confessed her failed attempt at getting a long-term lease for one of the cottages. Desiree promised that she'd personally take care of it, and had teased her with the amenities that only

The Port could provide. Olivia didn't need much convincing, as she sensed that not only would she find a great place to stay but had also found a friend in Desiree Davenport.

Her cottage at The Port was as close to a "home" as she could get. The single-floor design was set in a small cul-de-sac that looked out onto the beach. Floor-to-ceiling windows flanked the east to bring in the morning sun. A fully functional HGTV-worthy kitchen was complete with stainless-steel appliances, dishwasher and a stackable washer and dryer tucked away in a closet. The living area was simple but classy, with soft taupe furnishings, hardwood floors, a fireplace for those chilly nights and a built-in sound system. Her bedroom accommodated a king-size bed, cherrywood dresser and bureau, and a to-die-for walk-in closet. The bathroom was the perfect getaway, with a soaker tub and Jacuzzi jets and recessed lighting to set the perfect relaxing mood. To sweeten the pie, The Port was also a full-service establishment with its own restaurant and bar, day spa and gym, and Desiree and Lincoln had recently added a concierge service for any guests staying for a week or more. Olivia could easily see why The Port was so successful and always full.

No sooner had she opened the foyer closet to get her light shawl than the doorbell chimed. Her heart actually banged in her chest. She licked her lips, drew in a breath and went to open the door.

The light of a half-moon drew an outline around the striking figure that was standing in her doorway.

Olivia's lips parted but the words got tangled deep in her throat.

"I thought I'd surprise you."

"Victor . . . what are you doing here?"

"Don't look so happy to see me," he teased, apparently mistaking her horror for surprise.

An awkward moment of "what next" stood between them.

Olivia's gaze darted beyond Victor's broad shoulders, checking for Connor's car, which would be pulling up any minute.

"All dressed up for a night in?" he finally said, as realization dawned on him.

Olivia shifted her weight and folded her arms. "I would invite you in but . . . I'm expecting someone."

"I see. Always did have bad timing when it came to you." He raised his hands in supplication. "Totally my fault. I should have called." He studied his shoes for a moment, then sheepishly looked at her. "I'm staying at the hotel in town. Why don't I give you a call tomorrow."

"Fine," she managed to reply. She offered a tight-lipped smile.

Victor leaned down and pecked her lightly on the cheek. "Enjoy your evening. You look beautiful, by the way." He turned and trotted down the steps and walked off to his Audi.

Olivia didn't realize that she'd been holding her breath until she felt the vein in her temple began to throb. She pushed the door closed and briefly shut her eyes. "What the hell," she muttered.

No sooner had she turned away than the bell rang again. Steadying herself, she went through the process again.

"Hey," Connor said in greeting. He slightly tipped his head in the direction of the two-lane road. "Busy night."

Olivia swallowed and lifted her chin ever so slightly. She didn't owe him any explanations. "One of those days," she said offhand. "Ready?"

A shadow of a smile played around his mouth and his eyes darkened with humor. "As long as you are."

The air hitched in her throat. She retreated a step. "Come in. I need to get my things." She spun away and click-clicked across the hardwood floor. Why did he have such an unsettling effect on her? His voice, his scent, his movements, those eyes, his lips . . .

Connor leaned against the still-open door and watched her. Slowly he rocked his jaw as he contemplated the night ahead. Generally, he was a man who wasn't into surprises. Didn't like them. He planned his life much the same way he planned his jobs — with efficiency, always factoring in contingency plans, just in case. It was rare that he encountered "just in case" moments. Olivia Gray was one, and for the first time he had no contingency plan.

Olivia came toward him. "You didn't have to stand in the doorway." She tucked her purse under her arm and draped her shawl around her shoulders.

Connor stepped around her. She felt the hard heat of him against her back. Goose bumps sprouted along her arms. She shuddered. He pressed his long fingers onto her shoulders and gently adjusted the shawl, smoothing his hands along the fabric. "All set," he said close to her ear.

A flutter of need flapped in her pelvis and the warm dewdrops quickly followed. She moved away from his invisible embrace. "Slam the door and it will lock behind you," she said, and stepped out into the pleasantly warm night.

Connor opened the car door for her, then came around to the driver's side while humming an offbeat tune.

The interior of the Mercedes held his scent, which swirled around Olivia, fogging her clarity. She felt for the first few moments when the door closed that she'd been injected with an aromatic aphrodisiac. To offset her sense of almost weightlessness she forced her attention to routine: fasten seat belt, check lock on door, lay purse on lap.

"Hope you enjoy live music," Connor said, entering the safe space of her self-imposed sanctuary of banal activity.

"Most of the time," she said in a teasing tone, clearly referring to his attempt at humming.

He gave her a quick look. "Don't worry, I have no plans to quit my day job."

The tight line of tension in the center of her chest snapped with her laughter. "Good to know."

"I'm pained, *cher,*" he said, slipping easily into his Louisiana vernacular, the barely there twang only adding to his sensual appeal.

Olivia instinctively reached for his arm in a conciliatory gesture. *Bad move.* Her fingertips tingled above the tight ropes of his forearm. He flashed her a half grin. "Many are called, few are chosen, somebody important once said," she murmured.

"Killing me with kindness will get you kissed," he said, his voice low and sandpaper rough. He slid his gaze toward her, then back to the road.

Olivia tugged on her bottom lip with her teeth and slowly removed her hand from his arm.

Connor reached forward to the lit dash and pressed the screen. Something bluesy filled the air.

Olivia linked her fingers together. "So . . . what kind of music?"

"Local band. Heard they were pretty good. Little jazz, little blues. They have a soloist, and the food is great. I think you'll like it for a small seaside town."

"You say that as if you think I'm slumming or something."

He cut her a look. "Not at all. Simple observation." His fingers caressed the steering wheel. "Are you always so defensive?"

Olivia sat up straighter. Her fingers tightened around her purse. "I'm not defensive. I don't see how you could come to that conclusion. I was simply . . ." She felt his laughter more than she heard it, and then she heard herself, the echo of her defense bouncing around in her brain. She snapped her head toward him and caught the smirk wavering around his lips. She lowered her head and began to laugh. "I do sound a little on edge and full of myself," she ruefully admitted.

"If you say so," he teased. He made a right turn that led to the main road heading into town.

Olivia began to relax.

"Why do you think that is?" he asked.

"What?"

"Why you throw up guards and raise the bridge to the moat."

Olivia sputtered a laugh. "A moat? Really?"

"Bad analogy, but you get what I mean. No offense," he quickly added, his voice laced with humor.

"None taken."

"So . . ." He slowed the car, then turned into the parking lot reserved for the customers of Misty's.

"Old habits," she quietly confessed.

Connor put the car in Park, turned to look at her. "I know all about that." His light-filled eyes glided across her face. He unsnapped his belt and then hers. He placed the tip of his finger beneath her chin. "How about we start some new habits."

She swallowed.

Connor slowly moved toward her until the world disappeared and the sweet heat of his mouth touched down on her, and there was nothing she could do to hold back the moan that rose from the center of her being. He gently sucked on her bottom lip before turning away and getting out of the car in a single movement.

Olivia's heart banged in her chest. The heat in her head was so intense that it rushed downward and flowed through her limbs.

Connor pulled her door open, extended his hand and helped her to her feet. He pushed the door closed with his free hand. "Ready?"

All she could manage was a slight nod. Connor wrapped his fingers around hers, enveloping them, and led her to the entrance of Misty's.

The club was abuzz with activity. Many of the circular tables were full. The couple was quickly greeted by a hostess.

"Welcome to Misty's. Do you have a reservation?"

"Yes. Lawson," Connor said.

The young woman checked the computer screen then looked up at them with a bright smile. “Your table is ready and waiting.” She signaled to one of the waitstaff, who led them around the tables to one that was close to the stage.

“Can I get you something to drink before you order?” the waitress asked while placing menus in front of each of them.

“Bourbon. Neat.” Connor turned to Olivia.

“I’ll have an apple martini.”

“Very good. I’ll be right back with your drinks.”

Olivia settled in her seat and took a look around. “Very nice,” she said, taking in the intimate decor that was reminiscent of The Blue Note in the West Village in New York.

“I’ve only been here once before but it was a good experience — that I wanted to share with you.” The flame flickering in the glass centerpiece lit his eyes and made them sparkle.

Before Olivia could respond the waitress returned with their drinks. “Can I get you something to start?” She looked from one to the other.

“Maybe you could give us a few minutes.”

“Of course.” She spun away.

“Prompt service,” Olivia said with a chuckle.

“All the signs of a good evening.” He lifted

his glass.

Olivia did the same.

"To forming new habits."

Olivia's glossed lips quirked with a smile. She touched her glass to his.

Connor took a swallow of his drink. "So . . . tell me, what do I need to know about Olivia Gray that isn't on your very impressive résumé?" He studied the way her gaze slipped away for a moment and a brief shadow passed quickly across her face.

Olivia set her glass down and met his stare with one of her own. "My résumé? You've been checking up on me?" She wrapped her fingers around her glass.

He gave a dismissive shrug. "I always want to know who I'm dealing with . . . in business and pleasure."

She blinked against his directness. She would not let him rattle her, she silently swore. Clearing her throat, she replied, "Pretty much what you see on paper is who I am." That was as close to the truth as even she knew it. There was so much about her life that was a dark hole, a hole that she'd dug herself out of, and Olivia had no intention of taking that journey again.

"I find it hard to believe that a woman like you is no more than data and degrees. What do you enjoy . . . when you're not working?"

She tugged in a breath and dropped the armor back into place. "Good food." She grinned. "I think if I'd chosen another profession it would have been a chef."

Connor grinned. "Really? Favorite dish."

"Hmm, smoked salmon with my *very* special sauce, asparagus spears and risotto."

"You think it can top my jambalaya, Cajun-style?"

She tipped her head to the right. "Is that some kind of challenge?"

"Ready when you are." His brow arched.

"You're on."

"My place or yours?"

The conversation was clearly taking a swift turn in a dangerous direction, but Olivia repeated her mantra. She would not be rattled. "Mine."

"Say when and I'm there."

The waitress returned. "Ready to order appetizers?"

They both picked up their menus and simultaneously ordered the wine-cooked mussels. Over the tops of their menus their gazes connected.

"I think one will be sufficient," Connor said. He lowered his menu and got a smile of confirmation from Olivia.

The waitress hustled away.

"Great minds think alike," he said in response to their order. "Now, you were in the middle of divulging some intimate secret."

Olivia sputtered a laugh. "Oh, I was, was I? And here I thought you'd just agreed to a challenge that I can guarantee you will lose."

"A woman who doesn't back down. I like that. A lot." He took another swallow of his drink.

"What about you? What do you do in your spare time?" she asked, shifting the focus off her to get her bearings.

Connor leaned back and looked at her from beneath those incredibly thick lashes. "Not as much spare time as I would like," he confessed. "But one of my big passions is travel. I have that part covered with the jobs that I get, but what I really enjoy —" he leaned forward, rested his arms on the table "— is painting."

Olivia's head jerked back in surprise. "Painting? Really?"

He nodded. "Yep. I have a small studio in all of the homes that I rent while I'm on a job."

"I'd love to see your work sometime."

"My door is open."

"Why did you ask me out?" she asked, shifting gears again as Desiree's comment about Connor not dating wiggled in the back of her head, vying for attention.

Connor rocked his hard jaw from side to side. "It's not something that I do . . . for a variety of reasons. Mostly because I'm not interested in 'the getting to know you' conversation that happens over dinner and dates." He paused. "But *you* I want to know. And if you ask me why, I honestly couldn't tell you."

What did you say to something like that? "Honest."

"I try."

She tugged on her bottom lip with her teeth. "I guess I should be honest, too."

"All ears."

"I did a bit of research on you, too." She lifted her shoulder. "After all, a girl can't be too careful about who she goes to dinner with."

His eyes darkened. "What did you find out?"

"That you're a member of the Lawson clan from Louisiana. Your father is Paul Lawson. You have a sister, Sydni, and a younger brother, Devon. Your uncle Branford is a senator. You are very well respected in your field and you've done some of the most important restoration work of African-American artifacts and sites in the country.

And you paint." She grinned.

"I would say that I'm impressed with you, but that would be redundant."

Olivia squinted in mild confusion.

"Everything about you impresses me." His voice lowered. "Everything."

Olivia's cheeks heated. She lowered her gaze to her drink. "I don't know what to say."

"No need. Just an honest observation. I will say that I hope this will be the first of more evenings." He lifted his drink.

"You're certainly direct."

"I don't know any other way. I figure if I put my cards on the table it's the easiest way to see where others are coming from."

"Makes sense." She sipped her drink, then set it down on the table.

"And if I'm going to be totally honest . . . I'd tell you that I intend to make love to you."

The saying that your heart stops was true. For a hot second, Olivia couldn't breathe. As much as she may have had the exact same thing on her mind, she never expected him to say the words out loud, and so soon.

The corner of his mouth lifted ever so slightly. He leveled his dark eyes on her.

Olivia nervously licked her lips. Should she be offended or turned on?

The waitress returned with their appetizer. "I'll be back shortly to take your dinner order. Enjoy."

The timing of the waitress couldn't have been better. Olivia's thoughts were all over the place. Focusing on the food was the perfect distraction, until Connor made even that a sensual experience. He speared the meat from the shell of a mussel, dipped it in the sauce and slowly brought it toward Olivia's mouth.

Her lips slightly parted. Connor didn't pull his eyes away from her, almost as if the intensity of his gaze was speaking to her, letting her know to open her mouth, let the meat slide across her tongue, let the flavor burst in her mouth . . . let the experience become one with her.

Slowly she chewed, mesmerized by the steamy look in his eyes and the half smile on that luscious mouth.

"Like?"

She swallowed. "Yes," she managed to reply.

"Good." He turned his attention away and the heat down as if he'd only asked her for directions. He lifted one of the appetizers to his mouth. "Know what you want for dinner?"

Olivia blinked rapidly. *You,* she wanted to

say, but of course she didn't. "I'm thinking the sea bass. Have you had it before?"

"No. But it sounds good."

Olivia drew in a breath to steady herself. "What kind of things do you paint?"

"Nudes."

She nearly choked. "You're kidding."

He broke out laughing. "Yeah, I am. You should see the look on your face."

Her cheeks heated. She slowly shook her head and grinned. "You are hell-bent on shocking me tonight. Is that the plan?"

"Not exactly."

"What exactly is the plan, then?"

He leaned forward and lowered his voice, which drew her near. "The plan, beautiful lady, is to have a fabulous dinner, listen to some good music, have an after-dinner drink, take a slow drive home and see if you're up to what I plan to offer. And if you are, we'll be having breakfast together in the morning."

She was certain he could see the banging of her heart in her chest. "You're not only honest but seemingly very sure of yourself."

"Would you be interested in a man who didn't say what was on his mind — a man who didn't know what he wanted?"

"No. But I also wouldn't be interested in a man who assumes that he knows me or knows what I want."

"What *do* you want, Olivia? Honestly."

What she wanted Connor Lawson could not give her — answers to the questions that echoed within the hole in her life. No one could. That much she was sure of. She'd tried. "I want to have a nice evening. Get up in the morning and do what I came here to do."

He slightly pursed his lips. "Fair enough. One thing my daddy and my uncles always taught us was in order to please a woman you do what she needs and wants." He lifted his glass, which needed a refill. "To dinner and work in the morning."

True to his word, Connor stayed clear of innuendo and verbal seduction. Instead, he told laugh-out-loud funny stories about his various jobs, and tales of his large and outspoken family. By the time they'd finished their main course and the band was in full swing, Olivia was slowly developing a different and fuller picture of Connor Lawson.

One thing that struck her was that he clearly loved his siblings and had good relationships with his extended family. She envied him that as she listened to the tales of the Lawson cousins' antics all over Louisiana, from his lawyer-turned-champion-for-the-underserved cousin Justin — who finally settled down — to the elusive womanizing Rafe, who was hell-bent on living life by his rules, even if it drove his father, Branford, up the wall and back. Justin and Rafe's irrepressible twin sisters were Desiree and Dominique — with Desiree being a secret race-car driver and Dom . . . well, Dom was Dom. Their eldest sister, LeeAnn, had stayed in the family business and married her father's protégé, while the other movie-making cousin, Craig, was on the fast track for his first major film award. Connor's own powerhouse younger sister, Sydni, had gone all the way to Brazil to find a husband. And his brother, Devon, was determined to be a music mogul, which drove their father crazy. Connor told stories of his cousins and siblings with good humor and a lightness in his voice that was totally endearing.

All her life Olivia had wondered what it was like to have a loving family, people there to support you and your dreams, share family trips and holidays. All those things were foreign to her. She had no frame of reference for the things he said. It was like reading about a faraway country.

"Sounds like an incredible family," she said, pushing away her very empty plate.

"We're pretty interesting. I don't get to see them as much as I once did. But with so much social media we find ways to stay in touch."

"The band is better than you said they were," she said, wanting to quickly steer the conversation away from her own lack of family life.

Connor bobbed his head in agreement. "Yeah, I have to tell my cuz Rafe about this group." He returned his full attention to Olivia. "So what kind of schedule were you thinking about?"

"I was thinking at least three days per week. Say from ten in the morning until three or four."

"Not a problem. I'm usually on-site, but if not you can always hook up with Jake."

"That works."

Connor signaled for the waitress. "You want a refill or dessert?"

The evening was coming to an end. Olivia had set her terms and apparently he was going to honor them. Now she was having second thoughts.

"No. Nothing else for me. Thanks."

The waitress approached and Connor asked for the bill.

"I had a really nice time. Thank you."

Connor smiled but didn't respond. He

handed the waitress his credit card. Olivia fiddled with her purse.

"We'll be on the job tomorrow if you want to come by."

Olivia glanced across the table and the smoldering look in his eyes ignited a fire in her belly. Yet his tone was non-committal, casual and in stark contrast to the vibe he was giving off. Or maybe it was no more than her own wants and needs making her see things that weren't really there.

"I'll come by in the morning."

The waitress returned with Connor's credit card. "I hope you had a pleasant evening and you'll come back again."

"Thanks," Connor said. He stood and came around to Olivia's seat to help her to her feet.

He was so close. She felt the heat of him, caught the heady whiff of the bourbon. He draped her shawl around her shoulders.

"Ready," he breathed, close to her ear.

A shiver slinked along her spine. "Yes," she murmured.

Connor placed his hand at the dip of her back and led her out. Warmth spread through her. Her nipples hardened and she drew in air from between parted lips. It took all her concentration to focus on walking and not the feel of his hand on her body.

It had cooled considerably when they stepped outside. Olivia pulled her shawl tighter around her shoulders as they returned to the car.

"Cold?" She nodded. Connor took off his jacket and placed it around her.

Connor opened her door and helped her into her seat, then rounded the front to get in. Olivia brought the lapel of his jacket up to her nose and inhaled deeply just before Connor got behind the wheel. Her eyes fluttered closed for a moment.

"Seat belt."

"Oh, right." She fastened her seat belt and tried to clear her head.

Connor turned on the music and pulled off. Much too soon they were pulling into her short driveway. He cut the engine, got out without a word and came around to open her door. Olivia's pulse zinged in her veins. Connor walked with her to her front door.

Olivia turned to face him. "Thank you for a great night. I really enjoyed everything."

His eyes moved slowly over her face. He placed the tip of his finger beneath her chin and lifted it until she was looking into his eyes.

"We can do it again . . . whenever you want."

Olivia swallowed. Her lips parted and Connor moved closer and kissed her so lightly that it felt like a breeze, except for the heat that followed the contact. He pressed his mouth more firmly against hers and the tip of his tongue brushed across her bottom lip. Olivia sighed against his mouth and his arm snaked around her waist, pulling her firmly against him. She felt his arousal press lightly against her and her head spun. She wanted to have breakfast with him in the morning.

The simple good-night kiss slowly grew in intensity. She gripped his shoulders. He explored her mouth, nibbled her lip, teased her with his tongue and then, when she was on the brink of pulling him inside her house, he stepped back, stroked her cheek with his finger, whispered good-night, then turned and walked away.

Her knees wobbled. Her heart hammered in her chest. She wanted to stomp her foot in fury. What the hell? How dare he? Her breath came in short staccato puffs. A heartbeat away from being humiliated, she spun around, fumbled with her keys and stomped inside, slamming the door behind her.

Olivia pressed her back against the door and squeezed her eyes shut. "Damn."

CHAPTER 5

Connor stepped out of the shower and wrapped a towel around his waist. He picked up his shot of bourbon from the double sink and padded into his bedroom. It was nearly 3:00 a.m. and he was wide-awake. Sleep was the furthest thing from his mind. What he should be doing was lying in bed with Olivia Gray beneath him. He tossed back the remnants of his drink and set it down on the nightstand.

He couldn't wrap his mind around what it was about that woman that had his head so twisted. There was nothing spectacular about her. She was definitely easy on the eyes, smart, good conversationalist, professional. Naw, it was none of those things. Women like that were regular parts of his life. It was something else, something . . . that he couldn't put words to. She got under his skin. She turned him on like someone turning on all the jets on a stove.

Connor shook his head and dropped down on the side of his bed, draped his arms between his thighs. He rubbed his hand across his face as if that would magically wipe away the image of Olivia from his sight.

He could still taste the sweetness of her mouth, tinged with the flavors of dinner and her apple martinis. Thoughts of the feel of her flush against him made him hard with need. His jaw clenched and he jumped up and massaged the rise of his erection.

It was going to be a long night. He tugged the towel from around his waist, tossed the covers back on the bed and got in. He stared up at the ceiling, then at the tepee in the sheets, before he turned out the bedside light. Yeah, it was going to be a long night. The only saving grace was that he'd see her in the morning.

Olivia wasn't sure if she'd slept a good three hours. Throughout the night she awoke time and again, stirred by the erotic dreams of her and Connor. She'd turn on her side and the dreams would start again. She flipped on her back, her stomach, her other side. One encounter after the other followed her like a hell-bent stalker. She couldn't get away, no matter how many detours she took. Finally, when the sun rose she gave up.

She dragged herself to the kitchen and turned on the coffeemaker. Leaning against the counter, listening to the pot drip while the unmistakable aroma wafted in the air, she thought about her evening with Connor and the night without him. Would it have been so awful to have sex on the first date? They both wanted it. Besides, she knew that whatever this thing was between the two of them, it could never be more than temporary. When her job was done, she'd go back to her life and he'd be off to his next adventure. Anyway, every aspect of her life was only temporary. She'd grown to accept that, live with it. It was just the way it was.

She poured her mug of coffee, added two teaspoons of brown sugar and a splash of half-and-half. The first swallow hit the spot and reignited her cylinders. She sighed in satisfaction, then took her coffee into the bathroom and turned on the shower full blast. After her shower she'd go for a run, get her mind right, work off the sexual tension that still pulsed in her veins, then she'd head out to the site. And see Connor.

Olivia wondered what his night had been like. Did he think of her, dream of her? Probably not. Connor came from a lineage of men that could have what and who they wanted. There was no reason for her to spend time even contemplating the notion that he wanted anything more than a night of hot sex. A shiver of desire scooted up the backs of her legs and settled in the pit of her stomach. She turned her face up to the pulsing spray and let the steamy water flow over her. But nothing could wash away the need for Connor Lawson to fill the hot, wet space between her thighs.

Olivia pulled up to the work site and cut the engine of her car. She took a minute to compose herself, prepare to see Connor. The run had burned off some of the tension but now the anxiousness had returned. How would he treat her? Better question, how would she respond when she saw him? To compound her anxiety, Victor had left her a message insisting that she make certain that Connor used all the proper materials — oak, cedar, mahogany — to rehab the original structures. He wanted her to check everything. She heaved a sigh.

Clearly she couldn't sit there forever. She gathered her things, got out and trudged down the incline to the homestead. The crew was busy working and didn't notice her. She looked around for Jake and spotted him getting into one of the trucks. She walked in his direction.

"Morning."

He turned, cupped his hands over his eyes to block out the sun. A half smile lifted his lips. "Good morning."

"I was going to get started today. Did Connor — Mr. Lawson — tell you?"

"No. He hasn't come in yet. But you do what you need to. Can I help you with anything in particular?"

"Um, I'd like to start on the outskirts of the homestead and work my way back to the buildings." She cleared her throat. "I will be checking on the materials being used to ensure that they meet our criteria for restoration."

Jake's brow knitted. "We *always* follow the specs," he said, his warm tone turning cool. "You need me to go with you?"

"No. I'll be fine. I'm used to working alone." She offered a tight-lipped smile.

He extended his arm. "Take that trail. It leads to the other side."

"Thanks." She started toward the trail.

"I'll let Connor know you're here when he shows up."

She waved her hand in acknowledgment.

Olivia began by taking photographs and

then collected soil, rock and plant samples. She needed to put together as much empirical data as possible. Often something as minute as a tiny plant could provide clues to the past and the people. She worked diligently for more than an hour, becoming totally absorbed in what she was doing. And then she felt him. Behind her. She turned and gazed upward. All the air stilled in the center of her chest.

"Hey." He slid his hands into the pockets of his jeans. His warm, dark eyes moved over her.

"Hey," she whispered back. She brushed the dirt from her hands.

Connor walked down the short incline and knelt beside her. "What are you doing?"

She explained her goal and the process, while Connor studied her samples.

"So these pebbles and soil can tell you things, huh?"

She grinned. "You sound a bit cynical, Mr. Lawson."

"Not really." He twirled a blade of grass between his fingers. "I guess I never thought much about the smaller pieces of the puzzle. My focus has always been on rebuilding, recreating, not what it took to make it." He turned to her. "Guess that's where you come in."

Her eyes crinkled at the corners. "We all have a purpose."

"And we all know our roles and responsibilities."

Olivia flinched at the edge in his tone and knew instantly that it was a result of her conversation with Jake.

"And one of mine is verifying, at *every* stage of the reno, that *all* of the materials that I use on a project are the original materials, from glass to shingles and every cut of wood. I built my business *and* my reputation on authenticity." His dark eyes bored into hers. He pushed out a breath and softened his tone. "How about we both accept the fact that we know what we're doing."

Olivia pressed her lips together and the knot in her chest loosened. She could read that so many ways. "I could agree to that."

He watched her for a moment before he reached out and brushed a stray hair away from her face. His fingers lingered on her cheek. "I thought about you all night."

Her throat clenched. "So did I . . . about you."

Connor leaned closer. His hand drifted down from her cheek to rest for a moment on her shoulder before slowly tracing the rise of her breast beneath her white cotton shirt.

Her breath caught. For a moment her eyelids fluttered.

She heard his deep groan an instant before his mouth covered hers. This kiss was no kiss of invitation, or one that asked permission. It was immediately raw and demanding and insistent on having its way with her.

Connor cupped the back of her head, threaded his fingers through the wild tangle of her hair and pulled her close. His tongue dipped into her mouth, explored it, made it his own.

Olivia gave in, gave all. Her fingers pressed into the hard muscle of his arms to keep from floating away.

"I could make love to you right here, right now," he groaned against her mouth. He pulled away, stared into her eyes. "But I'll wait." He pushed to his feet and extended his hand to her. She took it and he pulled her up. "I'll let you get back to work." He turned and walked away.

"Damn," she whispered, as she memorized the way his jeans hung on his waist, and that easy swagger that made you say, "Hmm." How was she supposed to concentrate on her work after that? She touched her fingers to her lips. "You better not wait long, Mr. Lawson."

Connor strode down the hill and along the trail that led back to the homestead. He lifted his chin in greeting to several of the crew that he passed. He went straight to the office, and shut the door behind him. The heels of his work boots cracked across the wood floor. He banged his fist against the desk and uttered an expletive.

What was he thinking? Anyone could have walked up on them. Forget about what they may have thought about him. He'd put her reputation in jeopardy. He wasn't thinking with his head, at least not the one sitting on his neck.

He blew out a breath. He needed to get with Olivia and have her put out this fire so that he could go on with his life as if he had some sense.

By one o'clock, Olivia was hot, sweaty and hungry. She'd collected several bags of samples, took numerous photos and made her notes. She arched her back and stretched. She was done for now.

She gathered her things and began the walk back to her car. The hum and bang of construction had quieted, as the men were on their lunch break. Several groups sat on hoods of trucks or on crates, chowing down on thick hero sandwiches and guzzling cool drinks. Connor was not among them. A distant rumble thundered in her stomach. She pressed her hand against her empty belly and kept going.

Olivia opened the driver's-side door and tossed her bag inside. When she came around to the other side she stopped short. "Connor."

"You were going to leave without saying goodbye." It wasn't a question.

"I didn't see you on my way back."

He opened her door. "What are you doing tonight?"

Her pulse quickened. "Um, I didn't have any plans. Why?"

"I'll pick you up at seven, treat you to my famous jambalaya." He grinned and her knees weakened.

She rested her weight on her right side and looked into his eyes, which seemed to sparkle with bad-boy mischief.

"I'm sure I'll be hungry by then." She slid into the car and stuck the key into the ignition. She turned to him.

"What do you like for breakfast?"

Her nostrils flared. She pulled the door shut and slowly pulled away. "Wow."

■ ■ ■ ■

Connor watched her drive away with a self-satisfied look on his face. Tonight couldn't get here fast enough.

CHAPTER 6

Olivia returned to her cottage and dropped her bag on the foyer table. She spun around in circles, ran her fingers through her hair, then let out a whoop of giddy delight. She did her own version of twerking, then skipped over to the fridge to find something to eat.

No sooner had she sat down with her lunch of cream-of-mushroom soup and a three-inch-thick grilled chicken sandwich than her cell phone rang. She picked it up and frowned at the number on the face.

"Hi, Victor."

"I thought I'd call first this time. I was hoping we could get together sometime to-day."

Olivia stifled a groan. "Did you have a time in mind? I was just having my lunch."

"I could stop by now, or maybe we could talk over dinner. I spotted some pretty nice places here in town."

Dinner was definitely out. "You can stop by now if you want."

"Great. I'll be there in about a half hour or so."

"Sure," she answered halfheartedly. "See you then." She set the phone down. The call from Victor took the icing off her cake. Well, there was nothing to be done about it now. They'd talk, she'd bring him up to date and he'd be on his way so that she could focus her energies on the home-cooked dinner with Connor.

Olivia finished her lunch and set up her laptop on the coffee table to be able to show Victor the images that she'd shot so far, along with her notes and samples. She was in the middle of pouring a glass of iced tea when her bell rang. She crossed through the open living room to the front. Preparing herself, she drew in a breath of resignation and pulled the door open. She put on her best smile. "Victor. Hi. Come in."

As always, Victor was impeccable. He was the kind of man that you could never imagine getting dirt under his fingernails. Until he'd met Olivia and they'd launched into their brief though passionate affair, he'd never owned a pair of jeans. He had some on now, perfectly cut, just the right color, and looking as if they'd come right off the shelf. He'd opted for a pair of chocolate Italian loafers, an open-collared pale blue shirt and designer sports jacket. This was as casual as Victor Randall got, and of course he smelled divine.

Olivia stepped aside to let him pass, but not before he bussed her cheek with a light kiss.

"Looking well, as always," he said as he walked inside. He gave the space the once-over, then turned to her. "Nice. Better than a hotel."

"It has its perks. I set everything up in the living room. Can I get you something to drink, coffee, tea, juice?"

"Coffee would be great. I haven't reached my five-cup quota," he quipped.

"Be right back. Black with two sugars, right?"

Victor smiled. "You remembered."

His tone had a bit too much intimacy in it for Olivia's taste. She wasn't going to slip down that slope. She went into the kitchen and prepared his coffee and then joined him in the living room. She set the mug down on the table.

Victor was already scrolling through the photos. "Thank you," he murmured without looking up.

Olivia sat in the club chair.

"These pictures will make great archival documentation, Olivia."

She watched his expression and body language become energized as the wheels in his great mind spun. It was the thing that had attracted her to him in the beginning — his unbridled passion for his work. Unfortunately, that was where his passion came to an end. He was turned on by work. Work was his aphrodisiac. Beyond that, Victor was a gorgeous shell.

"I started collecting the samples from the surrounding grounds. I'll begin with the buildings this week."

"Good. I'd like to see everything first-hand."

Her stomach jumped. She crossed her legs. "Checking up on me?"

"That's the second time you asked me that." He looked across at her, tried to see behind the placid exterior.

"Second time you gave me a reason to."

He leaned back against the cushions of the sofa, crossed his ankle over his knee and looked at her. "I'm not checking up on you. At least not in the way you think."

"What way is it that I'm thinking?"

"That my interest is work related."

"Well, isn't it?"

"Not entirely."

She didn't like the direction of the conversation one bit. She folded her arms. "Meaning?"

"I came down here for more than work. I know that you are perfectly capable of handling this assignment on your own." He glanced away for a moment as if debating his next words. "I've been thinking about us."

"Victor —"

He held up his hand to stave off her rebuttal. "Listen to me for a moment. That's all I ask."

She pushed back into her seat and folded her arms again. "I'm listening."

"I know that we had a good thing at one time and it was my fault, my selfishness that got us off track. Much of it had to do with my own ambition, my tunnel vision when it came to work. But in the time that we have been apart . . . I realize how much I miss you and want you in my life."

Olivia slowly shook her head and said, "Things can't work between us, Victor. You're my boss and . . . we've both moved on."

He leaned forward to press home his point. "That's what I really came here to tell you. After this assignment is over, I'll be leaving The Institute."

"Leaving?" She frowned in confusion. "What are you talking about?"

"I was offered the position of chair at the Center for Archeological Research in DC. I start in a month."

Her mouth opened, then closed. This didn't make sense. Out of the blue. "But . . . I thought you loved what you did at The Institute."

"I do. But this is a once-in-a-lifetime opportunity. I'll have my own team. Pick and choose projects from around the world. I'll be working with some of the most talented researchers in the field." He paused. "And I recommended you to take my place."

Her back straightened. "What!"

He smiled. "I recommended you and the board gave their tentative approval. Your contract will be up after this project. It would be the perfect time to take you from the precarious position as a contract worker to a permanent one with your own department. You've earned it."

"Victor . . . I don't know what to say."

"Say yes, and I can make it yours."

Her heart thumped in warning. "I . . . I have to at least sleep on it."

"Of course. But I'll need your answer before I return."

"Right . . . of course," she said absently,

her mind spinning in a million directions.

"So," he said, then took a long breath. He zeroed in on her face. "We won't be boss and employee anymore."

Her gaze flew to his to see the light of invitation hovering around his mouth. *There was the catch.*

"We'll be free to see where things can go." He pushed up from his seat and stood. He stared down into her upturned face. "Think about it. *Everything.*" He walked toward the door. Olivia followed.

"I'll meet you down at the site tomorrow, say about one?"

"Sure."

He opened the door and stepped outside. He turned to her. "This is a good thing. For everyone. See you in the morning."

Olivia stood in the doorway and watched him drive away before she returned inside. *Director of The Institute.* It was a dream that always seemed out of reach. But now . . . However, she had a deep-seated feeling that it wasn't going to be as easy as signing on the dotted line. Victor did very little out of the kindness of his heart. He would want something in return. *Her.*

CHAPTER 7

The local jazz station played an old Billie Holiday classic, "My Man," while Connor cut and chopped the peppers and sausage and prepared the spices for his jambalaya. He took a swallow of bourbon as he worked.

He was truly looking forward to the evening. He didn't cook for many women and he certainly didn't invite them to his place with the real intention of getting to know them, spend quality time. But from the very beginning Olivia Gray was different. All his standard patterns of behavior had gone out the window. Deep in his gut he understood that Olivia wasn't the kind of woman that would deal with his half-ass way of engaging in relationships. Maybe that was the attraction.

Connor opened the fridge and took out the tray of deveined shrimp that had been marinating overnight and placed it on the counter. He glanced up at the clock on the wall. It was almost three. He placed all the ingredients in the slow cooker. By six it would be perfect, then he would add the rice and let it all simmer for another hour.

He strode out of the kitchen just as his cell phone rang. He tugged it out of his pocket, saw the name on the face of the phone and thought about letting it go straight to voice mail. But that wouldn't matter, not to Adrienne.

With reluctance, he pressed the green talk icon. "Yes, Adrienne." His voice was a flat monotone.

"At least pretend that you're glad to hear from me," she whined.

"How are you, Adrienne?" he responded instead.

"Better now that I hear your voice."

"I'm busy."

"I . . . was thinking about you. I wanted to know how you are."

"I'm fine, really. As I'm sure you are."

"I read an article in *Historic Restoration Magazine* about the work you're doing down in Sag Harbor. How is it going?"

"Going well. Day by day."

"You were always so modest about your work and your accomplishments. That was one of the things I really loved about you."

"Adrienne —"

"I just got back into New York for an, uh, project I'm working on," she quickly interjected, "and I thought about coming out there. Maybe we could get together for drinks . . . for old times' sake."

"Old times' sake? You're kidding, right? Nothing good could come out of us having a drink together."

"Why do you have to be so difficult? It doesn't have to be like this between us. We had something once."

"*You* had something once. *I* had something else. Look, Adrienne, this conversation isn't going anywhere. Take care of yourself. I've got to go."

"Connor . . . wait . . . I know I messed up. I know I did a lot of things that I can't take back. But I'm sorry."

"Apology duly noted. I've got to go. Goodbye, Adrienne." He disconnected the call before she had a chance to say anything else that would really piss him off. He shoved the phone across the counter as if it could somehow distance him even further from the sound of her voice.

He flattened his palms on the countertop and lowered his head as a whirlwind of dark thoughts and images of the past whipped through him. He wasn't going to let a call from Adrienne Forde ruin his mood. Not today.

Shaking off the effects of a wrong turn down memory lane, he adjusted his attentions toward preparing dinner. Thinking about the evening ahead brought the hint of a smile back to his lips and loosened the tightness across his shoulders. In all honesty, whenever he thought of Olivia he smiled. That was pretty rare for him. Not that he was stoic, but it wasn't often that a woman brought a smile to his face by simply thinking of her. He shouldn't be surprised. Everything about Olivia was different from any other woman he'd known — at least so far.

With the slow cooker under way there was very little to do in terms of preparation. He did want to run into town and pick up a couple bottles of wine before it got late. Although Olivia liked her apple martinis, he wasn't the best at mixing drinks. Wine would have to do for tonight, unless, of course, she wanted to join him for a shot of bourbon. He grabbed his car keys and cell phone, checked his pocket for his wallet and headed out.

"He's fixing you dinner at his place?" Desiree asked, her voice climbing in pitch with every word.

Olivia laughed. “Yes and yes.”

“Well, I’ll be damned. And you haven’t had sex yet?” she asked in disbelief.

Olivia rolled her eyes and shook her head. “No.”

“Humph. Well, whatever you put on that man you sure put it on good.”

“Desiree, you make him out to be . . . I don’t even know what.”

“Look, when I said that he doesn’t date, I meant it. He may do a dinner-out thing but that’s about it. The single women in this little town have been after him from day one. Nonstop. He barely gives them the time of day. You are special. Period.”

“It’s only dinner.”

“At his house!”

Olivia laughed. “Okay, okay, at his house.”

“And I want all the details tomorrow. Unless of course you’re too tired,” she teased.

“Very funny. Bye, Desi.”

“Seriously, though. Have a good time.”

“Thanks.”

Olivia put the phone down and mused over Desiree’s comments. Was she special? Guess she would find out later. In the meantime, she had some notes to transcribe and then had to get ready for her evening with Connor.

■ ■ ■ ■

Olivia took extra care with her preparations for her date, making sure that everything above and below the waist was coiffed and neat. She spent nearly an hour soaking in the tub filled with her favorite bath oil. When she finally got out her skin felt like pure silk. She stood naked in front of the full-length mirror that hung on the back of the door.

For a thirty-four-year-old woman, she still had it. Gravity hadn't taken over as of yet, and between the running around with her job and her weekly workout, she stayed in fairly good shape. Her tummy could use a bit of toning up, but she hadn't reached the Spanx threshold yet. Her favorite feature of her body was her legs. They were long and shapely. With her line of work she'd didn't get to show them off as often as she would like. But tonight, like the other evening, was her opportunity.

By the time she finished selecting the perfect set of undies, and putting on her new dress, it was almost six. *What if she stayed the night?* Should she be so bold as to toss a toothbrush in her purse and a change of clothes? Who was she kidding?

She knew she was staying. She was looking forward to it with a giddy anticipation that she hadn't felt in far too long.

It had been many months since she'd been intimate with anyone. She chalked it up to work. The truth was that she had no interest in anyone. There wasn't a man who made sparks go off inside her, or turned her on with a simple look, a smile or a touch. Until she met Connor.

She ran her hands across the rise of her breasts and down the valley of her stomach. She could barely contain her need to be touched . . . to be touched by him. But if she could wait this long, a few more hours was nothing. She turned away from her reflection and started to get ready.

Promptly at seven her front doorbell rang. As she shut the door and followed Connor to his car, she reminded herself one last time that whatever transpired between them was only temporary.

When they pulled up in front of his place, Olivia's heart was racing so rapidly that it was hard for her to breathe.

"Make yourself comfortable," he said, and extended his hand toward the couch.

Olivia took a look around. Totally male. Totally Connor. The rich dark tones and minimal furnishings spoke to the rugged side of him, the transient side. There was no permanence here. Two of his paintings hung on the wall. One was of the docks; the other was an oil of a woman with her back to the viewer as she looked out across the horizon. His name was etched across the bottom. They were good, really good.

Olivia crossed the room to where a stack of paintings rested against the wall. She went through the half dozen of them. They were mostly images of the town and surrounding area. Others where framed sepia photographs of what appeared to be early settlers.

"I'm working on getting those restored," he said, coming up behind her and offering a glass of wine.

She took the glass. "Thank you. Where did you find these? They have to be more than a hundred years old."

"In one of the buildings at the edge of the property. Most of them have been damaged by the weather and age, but —" he shrugged slightly "— something can be done with them."

"I agree. I'd like to study them, as well." She turned to him. He was so close. She could see the light reflected in the darkness of his eyes. She raised the glass to her lips.

"Your work is equally as impressive. You have real talent."

"Thanks. Uh, dinner's about ready," he said.

She sensed a nervous tension in him that was unfamiliar. It was in the way he wouldn't look directly at her, the way he held himself just out of reach. The notion that Connor Lawson was actually uncertain around her bolstered her confidence, made her bold. She took a step closer.

"Everything smells delicious."

He half smiled and took a swallow of his wine. "I take you for a jazz kind of girl." He turned away and walked over to the stereo system on the other side of the living room. "Instrumental cool?"

"Sure."

He sifted through the CD stand, selected several and put them on. The baleful horn of Coltrane floated through the space.

Olivia took a seat on the couch and set her drink down on the table. "How did things go at the site today?"

"I left everything in the hands of my foreman, Jake. No calls, no problems." Connor came and sat next to her.

"So are you trying to say that you slaved over a hot stove all day?" She angled her body toward him.

"Definitely." His eyes drifted slowly across her face. "You look beautiful. Did I tell you that?"

"Not today," she said softly.

"You do." He draped his arm along the back of the couch and let his fingertips dangle along her shoulder.

Olivia contained the shiver that latched on to her spine.

"More wine?" His index finger stroked the side of her neck.

Her lids fluttered. *What did he just say?*

He leaned forward, took the bottle from the table and topped off her glass. "Ready to eat?"

She swallowed. "Yes."

He stood up from his seat, plucked her drink from her hand and extended his to help her to her feet. Olivia placed her hand in his and his long fingers wrapped around her palm. Gently he pulled her to stand flush against him. Whatever nervous tension she'd thought she'd witnessed in him earlier was gone.

Before she could think or react, his mouth covered hers. The sweet taste of the wine burst in her mouth as his tongue refused to wait for permission to tango with hers.

Her sigh flowed through him like water rushing through open faucets. He cupped her cheeks and drew her farther into his kiss. The sweet heat of her wrapped around him; her scent short-circuited his senses. She made him crazy. There was no other way to explain it. And getting crazy over a woman was trouble and dangerous. He wanted neither, even as much as he wanted Olivia.

Connor broke away and took a step back. Without a word he turned away and walked into the adjoining kitchen. He had to clear his head. Some distance between them was what he needed.

"Thought we could eat in here. Keep it casual," he added, with his back still to her.

Olivia stood in the entryway of the kitchen, staring at his rock-solid outline.

"Have a seat." He lifted the lid of the slow cooker and the mouthwatering aroma of the jambalaya permeated the air. He brought the pot to the table and set it on the warming tray in the center, then he spooned the rice from a second pot into a large bowl and brought that to the table, as well. "I don't want to presume how much you want. One thing I can guarantee is that you will want more." He grinned but didn't look directly at her. "Help yourself."

Olivia hopped up on the high seat, thankful that it had arms that she could hold on to. Her entire body was still vibrating. Connor sat on the opposite side of the table.

They filled their plates in relative silence; instead of drawing them closer, the kiss had erected an invisible barrier. Olivia kept her focus on her plate, but she couldn't hold back the hum of pleasure with each mouthful.

Finally, Connor dared to look at her. He smiled with pleasure. His right brow arched in question. "Like it?"

"That would be an understatement. This is some good eating."

Connor tossed his head back and laughed and the tight line of tension between them snapped.

"Family recipe?"

"Yep, and a few things I've learned along the way . . . to kind of give it my own twist."

"If you ever give up restoration work, you definitely have a second career." She forked more food and chewed slowly, studying his profile. "So was it Mom or Dad's recipe?" She watched his jaw tighten and knew she'd inadvertently stepped on another land mine.

"My father wouldn't know a kitchen if you drew him a map. And my mother . . . Well, she wasn't around much."

"Oh . . . I'm sorry. I didn't mean to pry."

"It's cool. Part of who I am." He looked

up at her. "Used to it by now." He settled into his seat and leaned slightly to the side. "Grandma Sylvia — God rest her soul — taught me everything I know about cooking." He reached across the table for the unopened bottle of wine, uncorked it and filled their glasses. "Spent most of my summers at Grandma's house in *Nawlins,*" he said with a twang.

"Must have been nice," she said, working hard to keep the wistfulness out of her voice. She wanted to know more about him, his family, his life, but what she didn't want was for the conversation to shift in her direction. "Where did you go to school?"

"MIT."

Olivia's eyes widened with admiration. "I'm impressed. Not easy to get into MIT."

"Hmm." He shrugged nonchalantly. "I suppose."

"Education in general is getting more and more difficult to achieve. I really feel for the young people now. They will either be broken by student loan debt or not attend at all — at least those that don't have a college fund or parents that can afford to help."

Connor nodded in agreement. "The educational crisis is sad and all too true. I was lucky." He shifted in his seat, a bit uncomfortable with the idea of the deep pockets of his family that had afforded all of them the best education that money could provide. That was why it was so important for him to be his own man. His family had a legacy, there was no getting around that, but that was what he wanted for so many other African-Americans whose history was buried in the relics that they worked to restore. "At least this new initiative of free tuition for community colleges will help thousands of young people to get a start."

"Yes, there's that. What was your major?"

"Design and construction. But I went into the navy after graduation. I wasn't sure exactly what I wanted to do. My father wanted me in the family business so I hightailed it out of there." He chuckled.

Olivia giggled. "Why? What kind of shady business is he in?" she teased.

"Global marketing."

"What's wrong with that?"

Connor lifted his glass to his lips and took a thoughtful swallow. "Let's just say that my father's and my sensibilities are on opposite ends. I want to restore. His goal in life is to buy up whatever is available — land, businesses, people — and recreate them. My sister, Sydni, is his protégée. Fortunately she has a mind of her own and doesn't mind butting heads with him. But that's their thing. I do mine. Then there's my brother, Devon. He's the youngest, still wild, and loving the playboy life. You would never know just how brilliant he is by the asinine things he does. He was inducted into Mensa when he was sixteen. Called himself following in my footsteps."

"You're part of Mensa?"

"Yeah. Don't talk about it much, though."

"Why in the world not? I only wish."

Mensa International was an organization founded in 1946 for those whose IQs were in the top 2 percent of the country. To be a member was certainly to be included in an elite if not eclectic community of individuals. Olivia was duly impressed.

He grinned. "Most folks get the wrong idea, that because you have this crazy high IQ you're supposed to be ending world hunger or creating cures for incurable diseases." He shrugged. "Me, it makes me overthink things. And Devon just acts out, stays in one kind of trouble or the other. Drives my father crazy." He laughed at that. "My uncle Branford wanted me to go into policy analysis and work in some kind of think tank in DC."

Olivia put down her fork and leaned forward on her elbows. "I can't see you doing that at all," she said thoughtfully. "You have too much energy and you need to use your hands as much as your mind."

His gaze narrowed and moved slowly over her face as if he was looking at her clearly for the very first time. "The only person that has ever said that to me was my sister, Sydni."

Olivia lowered her head, then looked across at him. "I'd like to meet her sometime."

The corner of his mouth curved upward. "I think she'd like you."

They each had another helping of food before returning to the living room.

"I. Am. Stuffed," Olivia said, and flopped down on the couch. "Dinner was excellent."

Connor took a mock bow before sitting next to her. "Glad you enjoyed it. I usually go for a walk after dinner but we can skip that if you want."

Olivia angled her head toward him. "Don't get me wrong, I'm as much for physical activity as the next one, but not tonight. I am going to sit right here, relax and listen to this great music."

"Sounds like a plan." He settled back on the couch. "So . . . did you think about what I said?"

Her brow knitted. "Said about what?"

"Breakfast."

Her heart jumped. "Oh . . . breakfast." She ran her tongue along her bottom lip. *This had to come out the right way.* She looked straight into his eyes. "I take my coffee light and sweet, scrambled egg whites and whole wheat toast . . ." She swallowed.

His eyes darkened. "I think I can manage that."

"Something else Grandma taught you?"

"There were two things my grandmother insisted that I knew." He turned his body toward Olivia and stroked her bottom lip with his thumb. "How to cook and how to keep a lady happy."

"You have cooking down to an art form . . . the rest is still to be decided."

A lustful smile curved his mouth and he hummed deep in his throat. "A new challenge always excites me."

Her clit twitched. She shifted slightly in her seat. "Do I fall into the challenge category?"

Connor watched the column of her throat work and the tiny pulse flutter like a sparrow's wings. "Definitely." He leaned in and kissed her. Lightly at first and slowly demanding more until she was fully in his arms, totally engaged in the melding of their mouths and the mating of their tongues.

All he needed was to see her naked, touch her, push himself into her and expel this maddening desire he had. Then he could see clearly, think rationally and move on with his life. It took every bit of self-control not to take her right then and there on the couch as he'd done with others. But not Olivia. Not the first time.

Connor eased away and stood in one smooth movement. He extended his hand to her. Her skin glowed as if lit from beneath. He watched the rise and fall of her chest and the way her eyes caught the shimmer of light. His clenched his jaw. He needed her. Now.

"Come," he managed to say.

Olivia placed her hand in his and followed his lead into his bedroom.

Chapter 8

The moment they crossed the threshold, Connor wrapped Olivia in his arms and held her against him. He inhaled her scent, memorized the way her body shifted to merge with his. He had to taste her again and he did, with sweet nibbles along her neck, across her collarbone, behind her ear, her cheek, until he met her lips. The simmering heat that smoldered in his belly erupted and rose upward into a groan that flowed into her. With her encircled in his arms he slowly backed up toward his bed.

"This is what you want," he declared, his tone ragged with raw need.

"Yes," she whispered against his lips an instant before his tongue delved into her mouth.

Facing her on the king-size bed, Connor began his quest to conquer her body. Inch by inch he explored, ceremoniously removing her clothing to reveal by degrees the satiny coffee-brown skin that heated and fluttered beneath his mouth and his fingertips. When she was down to her lace bra and panties Connor took a moment to assess the treasure in front of him.

"You're beautiful." He kissed the rise of her breasts that overflowed the cups of her bra. Tenderly he caressed the fullness of her, then slipped the straps off her shoulders and the cups beneath the swell of her breasts, pushed them higher. A groan rumbled in his throat when he took one turgid nipple between his lips and laved it with his tongue.

Olivia's body tensed and arched as if stunned by an electric current. She gripped the sheet in her fists and let the thrilling sensation of his mouth on her body flow through her. Her soft moans only served to heighten Connor's desire.

Connor moved from one side to the other, then down to her stomach, where he toyed with her navel, then across to the line of her hip bones. That elicited a shiver from her. He secured her hips with his hands and moved lower, holding her in place. His tongue drew a fine hot line along her inner thighs until she was weak and whimpering. Her pelvis instinctively rose and fell but it wasn't time yet. He needed her to want him beyond reason. He wanted her body to commit to his before he entered her, so that every inch of her would respond to him. He wanted to erase from her mind and body any other man she'd been with, and make her his own.

Connor pressed the heat of his wet mouth between her legs. The heady scent of her rushed to his head. He almost came.

"Ohhh . . ."

With his teeth, he pushed aside the strip of her panties and teased the slick split with his tongue. Had it not been for the hold that he had on her she would have bucked him off the bed.

He licked, teased and suckled. All the while her cries and whimpers grew louder and more intense. Her body vibrated, trembled and seized, but he wouldn't stop. He needed her at the brink, right on the edge of release, that moment when she would beg him to take her to the other side.

His cock was so hard it felt as if it would break, and the swell of his sac was a sure sign that he wouldn't hold out much longer.

Connor leaned back and rested on his haunches. He unfastened his pants, stood and took them off, leaving them on the floor. His boxers followed.

Olivia held her breath when she looked at him. She reached out to touch him and cupped the throbbing phalanx in her palm. Connor's head tilted back and a hiss seeped through his clenched teeth.

She began to stroke him, relishing the heft and silken feel of him, the way his expression tightened in pleasure. She was beyond ready and she wanted him now. She sat up, wrapped her arms around his waist and took him into her mouth.

"Agggh!" He grabbed the back of her head to hold her in place and to give himself a moment to get control before he exploded.

Her tongue licked the underside of his shaft and the tease shot up his spine. He cupped her chin and eased himself out of her mouth. "Enough," he growled.

Olivia smiled. "I don't think so," she whispered. She scooted back on the bed and tugged off her panties. She spread her legs wide for him and bent her knees.

Connor muttered a curse, reached in the nightstand and took out a condom. He tore the packet open with his teeth and quickly rolled the thin latex down his throbbing erection.

Olivia's heart was beating so fast she could barely breathe. She watched him move over her, blocking out everything except the look of hunger in his eyes. The swollen head of his penis pressed against her wet opening.

Her body tensed. Connor slipped his hands beneath her behind and lifted her toward him. He covered her mouth with his and pushed deep inside her in one long thrust.

He swallowed her outcry and made her thrill his own. Slowly he moved within her. In and out, in and out until they both hit a rhythm that had them moving, grinding and moaning in ecstasy.

Connor kissed her mouth, the column of her neck, suckled her breasts and stroked her heated flesh, all the while giving it to her as if she'd been made love to by amateurs all her life. His strokes were long and firm, and at times he would rotate his hips just before diving in, which would set her body quaking. More than once he hit that spot and she nearly lost her mind.

Olivia raised her knees and tightened them along Connor's sides. She lifted her hips and thrust hard against him again and again.

His grip on her rear grew tighter. His fingers dug into the taut flesh. His thrust grew faster, deeper.

Olivia couldn't think. She was one raw nerve from the balls of her feet to the top of her head. Tears sprang from her eyes. Connor hit her spot again. She screamed.

"Oh, Connor . . . Please . . . please."

"Please what, baby?" he groaned in her ear.

"Come for me. Come with me."

"You ready for that?"

"Yes," she whimpered. "Yes."

Connor slid his hand down between them, pressed his thumb against her swollen, throbbing clit and gave her four deep thrusts that set her off.

Her nails dug into his shoulders as a scream of release caught in her throat. Her insides squeezed and convulsed around his shaft as he continued to move inside her. Her body was no longer her own. It was a sea of pure unadulterated pleasure.

Olivia gripped his buttocks and squeezed. Connor's entire body jerked, his head arched back and a guttural, incomprehensible sound rumbled from his lips as the very essence of his being shot from him.

CHAPTER 9

Connor collapsed his weight on top of Olivia and buried his head in the curve of her neck, breathing hard. She stroked his back, soothing and cooing as her body slowly began to return to her. His heart pounded in rhythm with hers and that made her smile. She could still feel him inside her, and the sensation inadvertently caused her walls to clench around him, eliciting ragged moans from Connor and reigniting his need for her.

He'd never completely lost his erection, and Olivia's vagina was doing crazy things to him. Before he could fully recover he was completely hard again and ready to go for the gold one more time, which Olivia was totally up for.

Connor lay on his back with Olivia curled across his chest. His free arm was draped protectively around her. In the dim light he stared up at the ceiling while he listened to Olivia's steady breathing. *That. Was. Something.* He angled his head and peeked down at her. Her wild curls hid her face but he'd memorized every angle. Sex was something he could have pretty much when he wanted and with whom. This — this thing that had happened between him and Olivia — wasn't sex. He'd had plenty, and sex wasn't what they had shared. There was a part of him, a part of his soul, that was worn and hollowed out much like many of the buildings he was called in to restore. So he went after sex as a way to fill the gap, repair the damaged parts. It never worked. But he kept trying. Sex and work, work and sex. This was different. He couldn't explain it. All he knew was that for now the echo of emptiness that resided in the center of his being wasn't as loud.

He inhaled deeply, shut his eyes and let the sleep of the satiated consume him.

Olivia blinked against the slim rays of sun that slipped in between the slats of the blinds. As she came fully awake her heart jumped when she realized where she was — in Connor Lawson's bed. Inch by inch her mind took inventory of her body. She was sticky between her legs, her thighs ached and her nipples felt tender — all a result of the most incredible night she'd ever experienced with a man. Her skin still tingled.

Connor stirred, moaned in his sleep. Olivia eased out of his embrace and as quietly as she could, slid out of bed. She went to the front room and got her purse, then tiptoed into the bathroom. She closed the door behind her. She opened a narrow closet and found it stacked with washcloths and towels. She took one of each and turned on the water in the sink, then took out her toothbrush from her purse. She grinned. Wouldn't want their first morning together to be highlighted by morning breath, she thought.

After freshening up she stealthily went into the kitchen and hunted down the coffeemaker, which was tucked away in the overhead cabinet along with a bag of coffee. Within moments the savory aroma of fresh brewing coffee filled the air. Olivia leaned her bare hip against the counter while the coffee perked. She folded her arms beneath her breasts and let her thoughts drift back to her night with Connor. Surreal was the only way she could describe what had happened between them. But . . . she wouldn't overthink it or allow even an inkling of "more than this" to enter her thoughts. Yes, it was great, it was mind-blowing, it was unmatched. But it was also temporary. In a matter of six weeks or maybe less she would be back in New York, and possibly taking over a new position at The Institute. She exhaled a long breath and turned toward the coffeepot.

"Fabulous view."

Olivia swung around. Connor was standing in the doorway, staring at her naked body as if she was to be served on a platter for breakfast.

Olivia blinked back her momentary embarrassment. She should have put something on, especially while she was wandering around someone else's home. But the appraisal and admiration that glowed in Connor's eyes and played around his mouth pushed any inklings of embarrassment out of the way. If anything, she felt empowered in her nakedness.

"Coffee?"

"Sure." He sauntered into the room, bare chested, and his lower half covered in a pair of black boxers. But Olivia knew all too well what treasure rested beneath. He sidled up to the table and took a seat.

Olivia took two mugs from the cabinet and filled them both. She set one in front of Connor, then sat next to him.

"How did you sleep?"

Her stomach fluttered. "Very well. You?"

"My dreams were very vivid, like a movie." He let his gaze skip over her face. "But then I realized they weren't dreams. They were real and we were the stars."

Olivia's cheeks grew warm. She lowered her head and stared into her coffee mug. "Award-worthy?"

Connor chuckled. "You have my nomination." He slapped his palms on the table. "I'm starved." He rose from his seat and went to the fridge. He opened the door and peered around inside. He turned to look over his shoulder. "How 'bout a smoked-salmon frittata?"

Olivia's eyes widened. "Stop. Are you serious?"

"Very." He grinned.

"Hey, go for it. Let me at least put on some clothes."

"Don't worry about it on my account," he teased.

Olivia rolled her eyes and darted off to the bedroom to at least find her underwear. She quickly put on her bra and panties and returned to the kitchen.

"I liked the *other* outfit better, but I have to admit it would be hard as hell to concentrate on cooking with all of the lusciousness on display." His eyes rolled up and down her body. He ran his tongue across his lips, then pushed out a breath. "Well, you can make yourself useful. In the cabinet by the door, would you get the olive oil, salt and pepper? And I think I have a jar of black olives."

Olivia gave a mock salute and went to gather the items, while Connor took out the eggs, salmon, a small onion, milk, heavy cream and cubed cream cheese. He brought everything to the table, then took out a large mixing bowl from a drawer beneath the island. He heated the oven to 350 degrees, then took down a skillet from the overhead rack. He lightly coated the skillet with olive oil and set it over a medium-high heat on the stovetop, added diced onion, salt and pepper, and stirred. Then he added the salmon and olives, and stirred briefly. "Can you whisk the eggs with the milk and cream?"

"Sure."

Once Olivia was done, Connor took the mixture and poured it over the salmon and onions, then stirred very lightly. He scattered the cubes of cream cheese on top and let it all simmer until the edges looked firm, then he placed the skillet in the oven.

He turned to Olivia. "About twenty minutes and we can eat."

"Smells incredible."

"I didn't get a chance to get to the market, so no fresh fruit. But I do have whole-wheat bread if you want toast."

"Toast is fine." She was more and more impressed with Connor with every passing moment. She prepared the toast while Connor set out the plates and put the steaming skillet on the island.

"Help yourself."

"You don't have to tell me twice." She reached for the knife, cut into the frittata and scooped a triangular slice onto her plate. Without fanfare she dug in for her first mouthful. Her eyes fluttered closed in ecstasy as the burst of flavors came alive on her tongue. She chewed slowly, savoring the mix of tastes and textures. "This is . . . incredible," she finally managed to declare.

"Thank you. Glad you're enjoying. Take as much as you want."

Between bites she stole glances at him. *A real Renaissance man.* Why was he unattached? There had to be some skeleton in a closet somewhere. No one was as close to perfect as Connor Lawson. At some point the shoe would fall.

"You planning on coming to the site today?" he asked.

"Yes. I need to go home and change and pick up a few things."

"I kinda like the outfit you had on last night." He gave her a wicked grin that cinched the corners of his eyes.

Olivia felt warmth spread through her, telegraphed from the heat in his gaze. She swallowed. "Yes, I'm sure it would be a big hit with the crew."

Connor chuckled and finished off his glass of orange juice. "Whenever you're ready I'll drive you home."

Olivia glanced at him over the rim of her glass. She could get used to this, sitting across from him at the breakfast table. She shook her head and scattered the image. "Great." She pushed to her feet. "I'm going to finish getting dressed. Breakfast was utterly delicious, by the way." She leaned over and kissed him lightly on the lips. "Thank you."

He scooped his arm around her waist and pulled her between his parted thighs. "Anytime."

Her heart thumped. "I, um, better get ready."

"You don't have to, you know. We could stay here today. I'm the boss. I can tell them whatever I want." He ran his hand down her back, then hooked his fingers along the band of her panties.

The hairs on her arms stiffened. Her breath hitched a notch.

He asked her the question with his eyes, and hers said yes.

Taking his cue, he eased her panties across her hips and down her thighs. Olivia finished what he started and wiggled out of them the rest of the way.

Connor reached behind her and unsnapped her bra and let the weight of her unbound breasts rest on his palms. Olivia's nostrils flared, sucking in air when his thumbs brushed across her still tender nipples. A tiny cry escaped from her throat.

Connor lowered his head and took her right nipple into his mouth, laved it until she whimpered and her fingers dug into his shoulders for support. He went to the other side and paid homage.

The muscles of Olivia's stomach fluttered. Her breathing escalated. She linked her fingers behind his head and thrust her chest forward. Connor slid his hand between her legs and teased the bud until it was in full bloom.

Olivia reached for him between the folds of his boxers and wrapped her fingers around him. Connor gritted his teeth. She exposed him through the opening and began to stroke him until he grabbed her wrist in a vise grip.

"Come here to me," he said on a rough breath.

Olivia didn't need much encouragement. She draped her thighs on either side of his, positioned herself above his high saluting erection so that her slick opening teased the swollen head. But Connor was no longer in the mood to be teased. He grabbed her rear, lifted his hips and pushed up inside her, knocking the air out of her lungs.

"So I'll see you later." It was part statement, part question.

"In about an hour or so," Olivia said.

"I mean later . . . this evening. I want to see you." He angled his body toward her and draped his arm along the back of the headrest. His fingers dangled down to her ear. He outlined the shell of it with his fingertip.

Olivia swallowed. "I suppose that would be okay."

"Good. I'll be here by eight. Need me to bring anything?"

Olivia couldn't think straight for a minute. "Um, no. Nothing that I can think of."

He pressed a button on the armrest and

her door unlocked. "I'll walk you to your door."

She threw him a sultry look. "I think you should stay put."

His lashes lowered over his eyes. "Are you afraid that I may . . . force myself inside?" he asked, the question ripe with innuendo.

Olivia puffed a laugh. "Afraid." She reached out and stroked his bottom lip with her fingertip and leaned close enough to kiss him, but didn't. "I don't think it's me who should be afraid, Mr. Lawson." Her brows flicked in triumph when she saw the smirk on his face. She opened the door and stepped out.

Connor depressed the button and opened the passenger window. "I'm always up for a challenge," he called out through the window.

Olivia glanced over her shoulder, then sauntered into her house.

CHAPTER 10

Driving over to the site, Olivia found her thoughts continued to drift back to her night with Connor. How was she was going to be able to pretend that nothing was going on between them while they were working together? As much as she was still walking on a cloud, the reality was that she'd gone against her own cardinal rule: "do not sleep with someone you work with." She'd psyched herself into believing that simply because it was destined to be temporary, it would be okay. She should have learned her lesson with Victor. He was the main reason she'd instituted her mantra. Now she'd tumbled right back down that rabbit hole.

She stopped at a red light and sighed. The real problem was that things between her and Victor were mostly surface and just sex, but that wasn't the case with her and Connor. At least she didn't feel that way. She shook her head, pressed on the accelerator and crossed the intersection. She was getting way ahead of herself. One night of mind-blowing sex did not a relationship make. Besides, it couldn't last. That was what she needed to keep at the forefront of her thoughts, and not get it twisted. That was how people got hurt.

"You're looking mighty happy today," Jake said when he stopped alongside Connor.

Connor glanced up from the blueprints he was studying on the hood of a truck. He half grinned. "Why would you say that? I'm always happy."

Jake choked back a laugh. "You happy? Man, you walk around as if you're hunting for bear every day. If I didn't know you I would definitely steer clear."

Connor's brows drew close. He knew he could be a taskmaster when it came to work. He knew he liked perfection, and he didn't mix business with pleasure. He didn't believe in crossing the line between boss and employees. That was when things could get complicated. So he kept his distance. But did his crew really see him as difficult or unapproachable? And if so, what made today different? *Olivia.* An inadvertent smile tugged at the corners of his mouth.

"See?" Jake pointed at him. "That right

there. Some kind of secret smile, as if you know something."

Connor shrugged. "Maybe I do." Jake was one of the few men that he could truly call friend. They'd been together for years and seen each other through all kinds of messes. Jake could be trusted. "It's Olivia Gray."

"You really think you needed to tell me?" Jake chuckled. "I saw that coming a mile away." He clapped Connor on the back. "Good for you. It's about time you got out of your self-imposed 'can't be bothered' routine and got back in the game."

"Is that right, oh, wise one?"

"You know I'm right. I'm always right." He dipped his head and cocked a brow. "Told you about Adrienne, didn't I?"

The muscle in Connor's right cheek fluttered. "Yeah," he conceded. "You did."

"Well, whatever you decide, go in with both eyes open. And think with the head on top of your neck." He chuckled at Connor's side eye, then leaned against the side of the truck. "Think it can go somewhere?"

Connor shrugged. "Hey, who knows? Probably not. She has a life elsewhere, and I haven't set down real roots in almost a decade. It is what it is for now."

He rolled up the drawings, clapped his hand on Jake's shoulder. "But knowing you, my brother, you will be the first to know and more than happy to tell me." Connor laughed and walked away.

Olivia eased down the slope to the site. She pulled to the side, cut the engine and got out. She skipped down the rocky slope to level ground, then headed toward the main building in the hopes of seeing Connor for a moment, to let him know she was around. Also, she wanted to get into one of the buildings at the end of the development and needed to be sure that she could gain access. She smiled and acknowledged the members of the crew that she passed, many of the faces becoming familiar. She walked through the "budding town," awed at witnessing the beginnings of life returning to a place whose history was longing to be uncovered. The single-storied structures were being meticulously repaired. Even though the buildings were hundreds of years old, the workers took great pains to match the new materials with the old. On each of the buildings there were waterproofed sketches or photos posted on the walls to indicate what the original structure looked like.

Olivia continued on to the main building. The door was closed. She knocked lightly, and when she heard Connor's voice, she stepped in, ready to toss him a saucy greeting. She stopped short in the doorway when Victor turned in the chair facing Connor and smiled at her. Olivia's heart jumped, then settled. She'd forgotten all about Victor's visit.

Victor stood along with Connor.

"Liv," Victor said in greeting. "Mr. Lawson and I were getting to know each other, sharing war stories."

Olivia swallowed her surprise, put on a smile and stepped in. "I'm sure he has plenty to share," she said, focusing on Connor in the hopes of being able to gauge him. But his expression was unreadable.

Connor came from behind the desk. "You two are more than welcome to use the office. I have some work I have to get to. If you need anything I'm sure Jake can help you." He barely looked at Olivia as he breezed by her.

"Nice guy," Victor said. He slid his hands in his pockets. "Smart, knows his stuff."

"I pretty much told you the same thing."

"I wanted to see for myself. I wanted to see what you saw."

Her gaze jumped to his. "What are you talking about?"

"You forget that I know you, Liv. Maybe

not fully, in the way that I would like again, but I do. And I heard it in your voice, and I saw it in your eyes when I came to see you."

She looked away and folded her arms. "What does any of this have to do with anything? I'm here to do a job. Period."

His eyes took her in. There was no mistaking the "don't touch me" aura that she was giving off. He cleared his throat. "Glad to hear that. I'm going to take a quick tour, make some notes and then I'm heading back to the city in the morning." He lifted his chin. "I need your answer about the position before I leave."

"I haven't had much time to think about it."

"I'll need your answer by tomorrow morning." He picked up his leather folder from the desk. "Have a productive day, Liv."

She watched him walk out of the door and a wave of anxiety rolled through her stomach. Victor had been the last thing on her mind when she was preparing to come to the site today. And after their talk at her house, she hadn't thought much more about the director position. Add to that the chilly vibe that she'd gotten from Connor and her day was off to a flying start.

Olivia shook her head in annoyance. This was the reason she steered clear of commitment. Well, one of them. She huffed and strode outside. She was here to do a job and that was exactly what she intended to do, and the boys could have a pissing contest if they wanted.

Olivia walked to the end of the development that bordered a small lake and a wooded area. There were hard hats hung on hooks outside the building, along with a warning sign of the dangers of entering the buildings without a hard hat. A flatbed truck loaded with slats of wood and tools was parked out front, but no one was around. She grabbed a hard hat, shoved her hair underneath it and secured it on her head.

Like most of the homes, the steps were dry-rotted and the foundation leaned to one side, giving the impression that the building was looking at you from an angle of curiosity. Gingerly, Olivia made it up the steps by holding on to the railing. She unlatched the door and pushed it open.

Dust and the scent of antiquity floated in the air. Flecks of the past danced in the dim light that filtered through the plastic that replaced the missing windows. Olivia put her bag down on the floor and examined the one-room space. It was much like the shack that she'd first seen with Connor.

Broken and dusty furniture and gaps in the wood floor spoke to the age of the room. She retrieved her camera from her bag and began to photograph the room. Then she began a closer examination, touching and pressing the beams. It was known that in many of these old homes there were secret hiding places where the inhabitants would store their freedom papers and other important family documents. She went over every inch of the room until she came upon a loose plank in the wall.

She squeezed her hand into the opening and her fingertips brushed against something firm. She struggled to push her hand in farther and her fingers wrapped around the object and pulled it out. It was a small bound leather folder that was cracked and discolored. Her pulse quickened.

She walked closer to the window to better see what it was. The folder was closed with a thin strip of fabric. The casing was so worn that she was fearful of it falling apart in her hands. She took a plastic bag from her purse and put it inside. Quickly she sat down on the floor, took a picture of her find and documented it in her notes.

The tingle of anticipation strummed through her. She couldn't wait until she got to a place where she could take a good, close look at the contents. With great care she tucked the plastic bag inside her tote. She took some more photographs and continued to examine the nooks and crannies of the room, but found nothing more.

After about an hour she closed up the shack and went outside. The atmosphere had shifted dramatically. The air smelled electric, charged. She glanced up. The graying clouds were pregnant with water and hung low over the rooftops and trees. In the distance the low rumble of an impending summer storm growled out its warning.

Olivia hurried back up the rutted path toward the center of the site. The crew was working quickly to pack up and secure the structures. She stopped one of the men to ask where she could find Connor or Jake.

"Up in the office," the man told her.

She went back to the office, knocked and stepped in. Both Jake and Connor were hovering over some sketches on Connor's makeshift desk. They both looked up when she entered.

"Looks as if it's going to storm," she said inanely, sensing tension in the air.

"Guess you better be heading home, then," Connor said, without looking at her.

Jake rocked his jaw but didn't comment.

"I think I found something. It was hidden

in a wall."

Now she had Connor's attention. He put down his pen and stared at her.

She dug in her bag and gently took out the plastic encased folder and held it up.

"What is it?" Jake asked.

"I don't know yet. I need to open it carefully so as not to destroy it or its contents."

Jake bobbed his head. "Great for you. Hope it's something interesting."

"I have a feeling that it is." She was talking to Jake but she wanted some kind of reaction from Connor. She got nothing. What in the hell had Victor said to him?

"Is there anything that you need? We really have to tie up a few things here before the storm hits," Connor said, still without looking at her.

Olivia's lips tightened. She drew in a breath. "No. Nothing. Get home safely." She turned and walked out.

"What the hell was that about?" Jake asked.

"Don't know what you mean." Connor rolled the blueprint and placed it in a plastic tube.

"You know what I mean. Just this morning you were almost singing her praises and now you act as though she gave you the clap."

Connor snorted. "Let's say that I got the real deal on Dr. Olivia Gray and I'm not about to get played again."

Jake frowned. "When? How?"

"Her boss — who is a helluva lot more interested in her than in the work that she does — is here on behalf of The Institute — the outfit that she works for. Stopped by to see me this morning. His laundry list of Olivia's attributes barely had anything to do with her skills on the job."

Jake's eyes widened. "Oh. And you believe him?"

"Why wouldn't I? His 'hints' were clear. They've *known* each other for years, he said. Worked very *closely* together."

Jake looked at him and shook his head. "Forget it, man. It's your life. I'm going to check on the crew, then head out. See you in the morning?"

"Yeah. In the morning."

Once Jake was gone, Connor plopped down in the wobbly chair. He ran his hand across his close-cut hair. All day he'd tried to get out of his head the things that Victor Randall had said about him and Olivia. He'd never come right out and said they'd slept together, but the message was clear as glass.

What did she see in him? He was an arrogant asshole. But the bigger question was did Olivia make it a habit of sleeping with the men that she worked with? Connor pushed back from the desk. What difference did it make anyway? It was just a sex thing between them. They were both adults. No ties. No commitments. Just the way he liked it.

Chapter 11

Olivia gathered her examination kit from the top of the bedroom closet. She brought it along with her camera bag into the kitchen, spread a special parchment paper on the counter and placed all the items on top of it. She took out two pairs of tweezers, white linen gloves, a magnifying glass, a video recorder and a small bottle that contained a preservative fluid. She dug in her camera bag and took out several lenses for extreme close-ups. Of course the technicians back at the lab would examine every detail, but she couldn't wait until then. She should call Victor, but she wasn't going to do that, either.

She set up the video recorder at an angle that would be able to capture everything that she did. Down the line, if this find was as valuable as she believed it to be, she didn't want any issues about authenticity or altering of information. Everything that she did would be documented. She looked over the contents on the counter, then slipped on the white gloves, turned on the recorder and carefully removed the folder from the plastic bag. She laid it down on the parchment, got her camera and took several pictures. She turned it over and took more photographs. With the smaller of the tweezers she carefully undid the knot from the worn piece of fabric that held the folder closed.

Her heart was racing and her hand shook ever so slightly. She drew in a steadying breath and with the larger tweezers slowly lifted the cover. The pages inside were worn, cracked and yellowed with age, but under the circumstances appeared to be in good condition. Ideally these papers should be examined in a properly air-controlled room to avoid disintegration. She should stop. The command ran in her head even as she leaned closer to examine the top page. She grabbed her camera and took a series of shots.

My God, it was freedom papers for Elijah Dayton and his wife, Sarah Hailey. Excitement brewed in Olivia's veins. This was a major discovery. Elijah Dayton had to be one of or *the* founder of Dayton Village.

What she wanted to do was tear through

the sheaf of papers, but she knew she had to move slowly. The slightest wrong move could potentially destroy evidence. Meticulously she examined the contents of the folder. She found Elijah and Sarah's wedding license. They were married in Virginia in 1890 and traveled north to Sag Harbor. It also contained the birth certificates of Elijah and Sarah's six children, Joshua, Luke, John, Matthew, Ann and Ellen, and their children's birth records. Elijah and Sarah had fifteen grandchildren, from what Olivia could determine.

There were other papers inside as well, receipts, notes and letters. The biggest find was what she was praying for. It was a receipt for $250. The receipt was made out to Elijah Dayton on July 6, 1891, for six acres of land, the land that eventually become Dayton Village.

Olivia plopped down in the chair. Her eyes scanned the contents that were spread out on the table. Her fingertips gripped the edge of the table. Incredible. Amazing. Tears welled in her eyes. Before her was the opening chapter of an untold story in American history. A free black man and his wife built an entire community that sustained itself for many years. But somehow, at some point, it all changed. The town virtually dried up and the people scattered.

Olivia used the tweezers to lift one of the grainy sepia-toned photographs for a closer look. It was the family photo of Elijah, Sarah and their children. The youngest was still an infant on Sarah's lap, and the others were stairsteps.

There was so much Olivia wanted to know. She studied each face. How had Elijah earned the money to buy the land? Where had the other townspeople come from? Where were their descendants? And why had the town fallen apart? So much was there, yet so much was lost; like her life. A life filled with holes and unanswered questions.

Each research assignment that she took on throughout her career was an exercise in personal discovery. There was always a niggling hope in the back of her mind that she would somehow find some connection to someone, somewhere that would validate her existence. She never did, but it never stopped her from searching and hoping.

She took one last look at the contents on the table before delicately returning them to the leather folder and slipping it into the plastic bag. She turned off the video camera, and was on her way to her computer to upload the photos she'd taken when her cell phone rang.

She looked at the name and number on the face. Her pulse kicked up a notch. She pressed the green phone icon.

"Hello."

"I wanted to make sure you got back safely. I didn't see you before you left and the weather is pretty bad out," Connor said.

So he did care. Olivia walked to the front window and pulled aside the curtain. The gray sky of earlier was nearly black. Wind bent the branches of trees while the rain fell so fast and furious that it bounced upward after hitting the ground. She'd been so intently involved in her work she hadn't even realized how bad it had gotten. She squinted and was able to make out dim headlights. Her stomach tightened.

She let the curtain fall back in place. "Wow, I had no idea." She spun away from the window and tucked one arm beneath her breasts while she held the phone in her other hand. "Thanks for checking up on me."

"Yeah, sure. Do you have flashlights? These storms tend to knock out the power around here."

"I guess I should check."

"I have a couple of extra in my trunk. I'm parked out front. I can bring them to you if you want."

Olivia grinned but kept her voice even. "Really? You're outside? Um, sure. Come in."

She felt like doing the happy dance but instead she casually walked to the front door and pulled it open, only to be literally assaulted by the whipping rain. Connor came running to the front door with a small duffel bag in his hand. The short run didn't matter. He was soaked.

"Come in. Come in. My goodness. It's awful out there. You're drenched. Let me get you a towel."

She darted off to the bathroom and returned moments later with a towel. Connor was already stepping out of his shoes and had tugged off his shirt. When he stood, wet and bare chested, Olivia muttered an expletive under her breath.

"Here you go." She handed him the towel.

"Thanks." He mopped his face and hair, chest and arms.

"Come on in out of the hallway. I can toss your shirt in the dryer." *If he took off his pants . . .*

"I probably should get out of these jeans, too, before I wet your furniture."

She swallowed. "Right. Right. The bathroom is down the hall on the left."

Connor strode past her and she caught a whiff of his scent that sent her libido on a wild ride. For a moment her eyes fluttered closed with longing.

Olivia walked into the living room. Connor returned with the towel wrapped around his waist and his soaking jeans in his hand. "If you show me where the dryer is I can just toss these in. Soon as they're done I'll be out of your hair."

"No need to rush." She came toward him and took the jeans. "The dryer is in the kitchen." She led the way.

"You were working and I interrupted you," he said, seeing the folder on the table.

With Connor's unannounced arrival that set her thoughts scattering, she'd totally forgotten what she'd been doing. The excitement reignited. Her eyes lit up when she turned away from the dryer and faced him.

"You won't believe what I found today," she said, sounding almost giddy with happiness. She hurried over to the table. "This folder contains the early history of the founders of Dayton Village! Birth certificates, marriage license, freedom papers *and* the receipt for the land."

"Whoa." His brows rose. "Can you show me?"

"I don't really want to disturb the contents

again, but —" she grinned "— I have an even better idea. You can watch me work."

He frowned in confusion. "What do you mean?"

She took the video camera from the table. "Let's go in the living room."

Olivia powered up her laptop, took the memory stick from the video camera and inserted it in the USB port. Within moments the images of her working on the folder and documents filled the screen. She and Connor sat hip to hip and Olivia had to force herself to concentrate on the images in front of her and not the fact that this man who she wanted for lunch was sitting half-naked on her couch. Did he have anything on under the towel?

Connor watched in rapt admiration of her precision and diligence. The process was slow and painstaking but she never seemed flustered. He could feel her excitement with each new discovery.

"So this is what you do, huh?"

She turned and smiled at him. "Yep. It's what I do."

"This is amazing," he said in awe. "You hit the jackpot."

She bobbed her head in agreement. "Yeah, I think so. And there's no telling what else may be out there." She sat back with a self-satisfied grin on her face.

"I guess that means that you'll be around for a while," he said offhandedly.

"There's still so much to do." She glanced at his profile and tried to figure out what was going on in his head. Did he want her to stay? "I need to do some interviews, examine the other structures . . ."

"Sure." He was thoughtful for a moment. "The Daytons and my own family have similar beginnings."

"Really? How so?"

"Well, my grandfather, Clive Lawson, was born in rural Louisiana, right at the height of the Great Depression. His father, my great-grandfather Raford, and his wife, my great-grandmother Mae Jean, worked in the cane fields. My great-grandmother started cooking for the people in the surrounding area and selling her dinners. They eventually opened a small juke joint. My grandfather was sent to work in the fields when he was ten. When the owner, Mr. La Fountain, died he willed a piece of land to my grandfather. Clive was only twenty years old and a landowner. Grandpa got his brothers to work the cane fields. They built on the land, made money, married and continued to expand. The story goes that they made their real money selling hooch."

Connor chuckled. “Guess that’s why us Lawsons love our hard liquor. The main house was built right where those cane fields used to be and it’s still there. It’s where we all grew up.”

Olivia listened intently, imagining the young Lawsons working the fields and building a family and a legacy. How she envied that, the knowledge of knowing who you were, where you’d come from.

Connor was contemplative. It was the first time he’d actually shared that part of his family history. There was never anyone in his life that he wanted to have know him in that way. Not even Adrienne. Yet here he was, throwing back the veil to a woman that he’d recently met. He glanced at Olivia. But she wasn’t like anyone else. That was the problem.

Olivia slapped her thighs and jumped up from her seat. “I am being a lousy hostess. Can I get you anything? Something to drink, eat?”

“I’ll have whatever you’re having.”

Her heart thumped. “Wine.”

“Sure.”

She went to the kitchen to get glasses and the wine from the cabinet. When she turned, Connor was standing there.

“I want to apologize about earlier.”

"Nothing to apologize for."

"Yeah, there is. I was being a real jerk."

She drew in a breath. "Okay. I can accept that," she said with a wry smile. "You want to tell me why you were overcome with jerkiness?"

Connor lowered his head and chuckled. "Victor Randall seemed to bring it out in me." He looked at her. "I have no right to feel one way or the other about you and him."

"There is no me and him." She paused. "There was once upon a time, but it never amounted to anything."

Connor leaned against the frame in the door and let his eyes wander all over her. "You sure about that?"

She swallowed. "Very." She took a step toward him and stopped. "Why don't you let me prove it to you."

"How?"

"Take off the towel."

His eyes flashed for an instant. "Right here?"

"Yeah," she said on a breath of need. "Right here."

"Pleasing a woman is what I do." He unwrapped the towel and let it fall to the floor.

The air stuck in Olivia's lungs. He had

nothing on under that towel. She toed off her shoes, unfastened the button on her jeans, unzipped and shimmied out of them. Connor didn't move. She tugged her T-shirt over her head and tossed it aside.

"Don't stop now."

Olivia licked her bottom lip, then reached behind herself to unfasten her bra. She swung the strap on her finger, then tossed the garment across the countertop, earning her a rousing applause. She giggled, turned her back to him, bent at the waist and rotated her hips before easing her panties across her hips and down her thighs.

"Woman . . ." he groaned, lusting after that perfect derriere.

Olivia turned to him. Her arm demurely covered her breasts and her free hand covered the triangular patch of hair between her legs.

She catwalked toward him, pressed against him. His erection was stiff against her belly. She felt it jump and she smiled.

Connor grabbed her, clasped his hand behind her head and brought her mouth to his. His hot tongue dived into her mouth, played there before he moved to her neck, behind her ears. His hands stroked her, tugged hers away from her breasts and her sex. He slid a finger into the wet slit and she cried out. Her inner thighs trembled.

"Aaah . . ." he moaned in her ear. "Almost ready for me."

She cupped her breast in her hand and offered it up to him, and he gladly took it. Her breathing escalated. Tremors shot through her body. She needed him. Now. She was beyond ready. She took him in her palm and massaged the head of his erection, then pressed it to her wet opening.

A guttural sound rumbled in his throat. He pushed her against the wall. His eyes burned into hers. "This is what you want?"

"Yesss."

"Tell me."

"It's what I want. I want you."

As if she weighed no more than a loaf of bread he lifted her and she wrapped her legs greedily around his waist, and then there he was inside her and she nearly came with the first stroke.

Olivia buried her face in his neck and held on tight as he moved her up and down on him at will. He cupped her behind and plowed harder and faster. Her head was spinning. She was so close. Her toes curled. Her head arched backward.

Connor drew a taut nipple between his teeth and sucked. Olivia screamed and her entire body shuddered when his finger stroked her from behind, pressed, and she exploded into a million pieces.

He held her, let her climax wash over her. His was on the way. His sacs were ready to burst. He pulled out with an animalistic groan and spent himself all over her belly and down her thighs.

They slid down to the floor in an exhausted heap.

Chapter 12

The fire shimmered in the electric fireplace, casting off a comfortable warmth. The rain continued to pound. Two empty wineglasses sat on the coffee table. Etta James crooned "At Last" in the background.

Olivia was wrapped in Connor's arms with a throw from the couch covering them. Connor tenderly stroked her curls, and placed tiny kisses every so often on her forehead. What she felt right then at that moment was a closeness that she had never experienced. The lyrics to the song were hauntingly real for her. She wanted to hold on to this moment, even though she knew it was only temporary. She snuggled closer.

"Cold?" he whispered.

"No."

He adjusted the throw over her shoulders. "What is it, then?" He ran the tip of his finger along the tiny cleft in her chin.

She released a slow breath. How much

could she say, if anything at all? But if she wanted to hang on to this temporary closeness she would have to give a little.

"You're very lucky, you know," she began slowly.

"Lucky? How do you mean?"

"You know who you are, who your family is, where you came from . . ."

He listened to the wistful quality in her voice and waited for the rest.

"I don't have any of that. I suppose that's what steered me into my profession, searching for beginnings."

"You want to tell me what you mean?"

Silence hung between them and stretched. Connor figured that was all she would say, and he wouldn't press her. Then she started to talk again.

"I have no idea who my parents are. I was . . . given up as a baby. Spent the first sixteen years in foster care. I did have some nice families," she quickly added. "I stayed with Frank and Lorna Hollis the longest. All they ever told me was that my birth mother's last name was Gray. They wanted to adopt me, but I didn't want it."

"Why?"

"I didn't believe that being adopted would change anything for me. Not really. I'd been bounced around for so long. As soon as I got attached I got pulled from the home and sent somewhere else. I didn't want to love the Hollises. I figured that even if they adopted me, at some point they would get tired, too. I couldn't deal with that. The only thing that was constant in my life was that I lived in Atlanta for most of it, until I moved to New York."

"I'm sorry," Connor whispered.

"Don't be. I'm used to it."

"Are you really?" He adjusted his body and sat halfway up. He looked into her upturned face.

"Most of the time I don't think about it much." She glanced away.

"And when you *do* think about it?"

She paused. "Then I remember that nothing is permanent. That commitment is overrated. That love is only for the moment. And if you love too long it gets taken away."

Connor didn't know how to respond, how to heal what hurt her inside or if he even could. He totally understood her reluctance to commitment; he had his own, as well. What was hard for him to grasp was not having family, a real one. Sure, he might be at odds with his father and might not be as close to his siblings and cousins as he once was, but he knew that come hell or high water they were there for each other. Family was the centerpiece of what made him the man that he had become.

He tenderly kissed the top of Olivia's head. For now all he could do was hold her and make the time that they did have together good times.

"Well, I don't have the fixings for jambalaya, but I can make a mean roasted chicken," Olivia announced as she came out of the bathroom freshly showered.

Connor had finished his shower and was putting on his dry clothes. "Sure. Maybe we can catch a movie or something afterward. It's still early." He tugged his shirt over his head.

"I'd like that. Sounds as if the rain has slowed down." She ruffled her wet hair with the towel.

"Need some help in the kitchen? I've been known to be quite handy."

Olivia laughed. "Of course. Can you cut and steam vegetables?"

He extended his arms. "I'm your man."

She wouldn't read anything into the words. "Come on, then." She waved him on.

They laughed and talked about all sorts of things as they prepared dinner: music, politics, religion and the places they'd traveled. The more they talked the more they realized that they had been crossing each other's paths for years. They had both been at Luther Vandross's last concert at Radio City Music Hall; they loved Lela James and had been at the New Jersey Performing Arts Center when she'd performed with Kem. When Connor stayed in New York, he often frequented the Akwaaba Mansion bed-and-breakfast in Bedford Stuyvesant, Brooklyn, and her first apartment was right around the corner from it. They'd both attended the same lecture series featuring Chimamanda Ngozi Adichie at the Schomburg Center for Research in Black Culture, only on different dates.

"I visited Germany about four years ago," Connor said, before taking a sip from his glass of wine. "There is always so much talk and data on the Holocaust but very little if anything is known about the blacks who were also there and tortured and experimented on."

"Yes! The Rhineland Bastards, they were called."

A spark of admiration lit Connor's eyes. "You know your stuff."

"It's what I do," she said with a grin.

He lifted his glass and she did the same. "To knowing our history."

Olivia tapped her glass against his. If only that were true.

After dinner Olivia felt a little lazy, a little cozy, and pleaded to stay in and find something to watch on TV instead. Connor agreed, with the caveat that she join him before sunrise for his morning run.

"If I blink my eyes three times and wiggle my nose will you go away?" she said, taken aback by the very idea of running before dawn.

Connor tossed his head back and laughed, then focused on her in all seriousness. "You're going to have to do a helluva lot more than that." He leaned forward, lifted her chin with the tip of his finger and placed a soft kiss on her lips. "Trust me. You'll love it."

When he looked at her like this, when he was this close, it was hard to deny him anything. She swallowed. "Fine."

"And since I'm such a compromising kinda guy, you can pick the movie."

The movie wound up watching them after they launched into another heady conversation. Connor told her about his very first reno job. It was a former brothel in the French Quarter and the new owners had wanted it rehabbed and turned into a tourist attraction.

Olivia giggled. "My first real job was in Atlanta. I was fresh out of college. I worked at the High Museum and I assisted the curator in collection and archiving. It was very interesting work. I stayed about two years."

"How did you wind up at The Institute?"

"Hmm. A series of opportunities presented themselves over the years. Internships. Postgraduate work. Fellowships. I attended conferences and met a host of people in the field. I got a recommendation from a fellow attendee when an associate position opened at The Institute. I didn't get it, but I did get a five-year research contract. It gave me some stability but I knew there was always an out."

"That's where you met Victor."

"Yep. He was my boss. What a cliché, huh?"

"It happens."

"He's leaving The Institute in a month," she quickly said. "He's submitted my name to take his place and the board has pretty much approved. All I have to do is say yes."

Connor sat up straighter. "Well, you're going to say yes, aren't you?"

"I'm not sure why I've hesitated to give

him my answer. Well, that's a small lie. I do know."

Connor's expression tightened. "Why?"

How could she put this so that it didn't sound as trite and trifling as it had become? "One of the myriad reasons why Victor and I didn't work is *because* he was my boss. It was wrong on so many levels."

"And . . ."

She pushed out a breath. "Now he feels that there can be something between us because we won't be working together anymore."

Connor's jaw tightened. He pushed up from the couch and crossed the room, putting the coffee table between them. "Can there be?"

She vigorously shook her head. She looked into his eyes. "No. It's over. Done."

"Then, why hesitate? What string is he pulling?" The lines around Connor's eyes tightened.

"Basically, if I say yes to him and me, it will ensure that I get the job. If I say no to a relationship, the offer will likely disappear. He didn't come right out and say it, but I got the message. So I'd be pretty much out of a job. My contract is due to end when this project is over. If I did decline the job offer and wanted to stay at The Institute,

I'm pretty sure that Victor would have a hand in not getting my contract renewed."

Connor murmured an expletive under his breath. His expression turned ominous. He wasn't going to go down this path. Made no sense for him to get his back up about some woman and her former lover slash boss and their happily-ever-after. "You'll figure it out." He turned his back to camouflage the dark turn of emotions that she would easily detect in his eyes. He refilled his glass of wine. "More wine?"

Olivia felt stung as surely as if she'd been struck. She wasn't even sure why she'd told him, why he needed to know anything about the decisions that she had to make for *her* life. That was what happened when you got comfortable, trusted, let your guard down. "Sure. More wine sounds great."

The movie ended. Dinner was over. The rain stopped. Conversation had dwindled down to awkward.

Connor stood, stretched. "I should be getting home."

"Oh. Sure." Olivia got up, rubbed her hands down her thighs. "I'll, uh, walk you to the door."

"Dinner was great," he said at the threshold. "We'll have to swap recipes."

"I'd like that." Her throat felt so tight.

Connor hesitated. "Olivia . . ."

"He doesn't mean anything. He never did. I don't know if it matters to you, but I need you to know that."

Connor ran his tongue along his bottom lip. He nodded. "Thanks."

"I guess that was a good way to get out of running before dawn," Olivia said with a half smile.

Connor stepped up to her and slid his arm around her waist, pulled her close. "I'm going to go home, throw some things in a bag and then I'll be back. We'll talk, drink more wine, make more love and before dawn . . ." He leaned down and lightly kissed her. "You good with that?"

She swallowed over the swell of emotion that lodged in her throat. "I'm good with that," she whispered.

"See you in about an hour."

Olivia stood in the doorway until Connor had driven off. This was scary. She was afraid — afraid of the steamrolling emotions that were hell-bent on running her over. Her eyes filled and she quickly blinked away the water. She couldn't risk connecting, feeling, being a part of something that was destined to end. She closed the door and turned away. It was too late.

Chapter 13

It was still dark. Olivia snuggled down farther beneath her covers.

"Oh, no you don't. Wake up, sleepyhead."

Olivia groaned and blinked until she brought Connor into focus. "It's dark," she whined.

"It won't be for long. Come on."

"I used to like you," she groaned, and threw the covers off.

"I'm wounded. I'll meet you in the kitchen. I put on some coffee."

She stuck out her tongue and tromped off to the bathroom.

After a quick cup of coffee they headed out. The world was still asleep. There was no rustle in the trees nor the melody of birds. Every now and again they passed a house with a tiny light in a window. Beyond that the two of them were entirely alone in the world as they slowly jogged along the path that led to the beach. An incredible sense of closeness enveloped Olivia, even more so than having Connor inside her body. The two of them against the world. A calm settled over her.

The air was crisp as a starched shirt, with a fresh-washed smell from the rain. The grass shimmered in the faint light that was beginning to awaken.

"You okay?" Connor asked.

"Yes . . . I am," she said, and meant it.

Connor took her hand as they made a turn. Just beyond the rise the scent of salt water rose to meet them. They cleared the rise, and what appeared to be an uncharted world spread out before them.

Hovering like a halo above the gently rolling water the fledgling beams of gold and orange fanned out, tinting the sea a color she'd never before seen. They continued down the rise toward the sandy shore and along the beach.

Inch by inch a new day made its presence known, rising in a glorious ball of liquid fire. Olivia's breath caught at the magnificence of the dawning. She slowed, stopped, captivated.

Connor smiled at the expression of wonder on her face and the way that the building light was reflected in her eyes.

"I've never seen a sunrise like this," she said in a faraway voice. It was a feeling like none that she'd experienced before, almost spiritual.

"It's quite amazing," Connor said. "Makes you realize how insignificant we are with our petty troubles and silly agendas in the face of this kind of awesomeness."

Her fingers tightened around his hand. Something inside her shifted. She turned to him. "Thank you," she whispered.

He leaned down and kissed her forehead. "Anytime." He jutted his chin toward the stretch of beach. "Come on."

"I'm going to head home first. Are you coming out to the site today?"

Olivia tucked her T-shirt into the waistband of her jeans. "I plan to a bit later. I have some writing that I need to get done and some calls to make."

"Have you decided what you're going to do about the job offer?" He picked up his cell phone from the nightstand and slid it in the front pocket of his jeans.

She released a long breath. "I'm going to take the job if the offer is still open, with the understanding that it's strictly business and nothing more."

"How do you think he'll take it?"

"Victor isn't a man who takes kindly to being told no. But I don't think he'd sacrifice a good business decision in order to stroke his ego."

"So will this mean that you'll be anchored in New York?"

"For the most part, but I will get to do some traveling."

"Are you going to be okay with that? Seeing the world from behind a desk isn't what you do, but maybe I'm wrong. I see you in the trenches."

For a moment she was taken aback. Would she be satisfied overseeing projects and a staff rather than being up close and personal uncovering history? She'd spent most of her life searching and looking and hunting and seeking. Maybe it was time to see the trees instead of the forest.

"Maybe it's time for a new beginning."

Connor studied her tentative expression. "Be sure it's what you want. Everything that glitters . . ."

She half smiled. "I'll keep that in mind."

He stepped up to her and pulled her close, lowered his head and gave her a slow, deep kiss that took her breath away. "See you later," he murmured against her mouth.

All she could manage was a nod of her head.

■ ■ ■ ■

Before she got too busy with the technical part of her job, she went through the house picking up and putting back. She stacked the dishwasher and put a load of clothes in the washing machine. Just as she was settling down to work her phone rang.

"Victor, hello."

"I was hoping to hear from you before I had to leave. Have you come to a decision about the job?"

She steeled herself for his response. "I have."

"And?"

"I appreciate the offer. I'm honored. But I'm not going to accept it." And the moment the strange-sounding words were out of her mouth she wondered where they'd come from. Yet in the same breath of surprise there was a feeling of relief.

Silence hung between them. Olivia could see Victor's cool sandy-toned skin deepening in color.

"I see. Well, no, I don't see. This is a big career move for you. From there you could write your own ticket, seek out projects and get the funding. Think about all the good you could do."

"I know. Believe me, I do."

"Then, what the hell is it? Is it because of what I said about us? Don't let your pride get in the way of —"

"Actually, no. Initially, I was going to accept the position and make it clear that it could only be business between us."

"What changed?"

She thought about the question and the real implications of it. She thought about what Connor had said and the truth that was in his words. "I know I wouldn't be happy going to meetings and worrying about budgets. It's not what I got into this for."

"Is there anything that I can do to change your mind? I'm sure the board would pay you whatever salary you asked for."

"The old 'money is no object' ploy," she said, tongue in cheek.

"That's not what I meant. Well, if you've made up your mind there isn't much more to say, is there? I hope you won't regret this later."

She could feel his frustration in the clipped sound of his voice and decided to let the comment slide. "Do you have any idea who else might be considered?"

"There were a few names tossed around. I'll know more when I get back and let them know of your decision to turn them down."

Olivia winced at the barb. "Have a safe trip, Victor. And thank you, really, for everything."

"I'll be in touch." He disconnected the call.

Olivia sighed. Hopefully, she'd made the right decision. Deep in her spirit she believed that she had. As much as she had combed the globe in search of solving the mysteries of the world, she knew she could never stop searching. Uncovering the past, traveling in search of answers kept the emptiness of her past at bay. She wasn't quite ready to give up the sanctuary of the hunt and be forced to face the abyss of her life, no matter how tempting the prestige or how high the salary.

She returned her attention back to the work at hand: clearly documenting the items that were contained in the leather folder. She took out her notebook, where she'd written down what she'd found and all the steps she'd taken, and transcribed that onto a computer file, which she then emailed to The Institute. She studied the images once again on the computer and tried to imagine what life must have been like for the Dayton family. What were they like and where had the family scattered? Why had they not wanted to maintain their history?

It was hard for her to grasp the notion that anyone with a legacy this impactful, one that changed the course of people's lives, would not care about preserving it. Yet she shouldn't be surprised. She saw it often, especially in areas that were predominately black. The stately brownstones in New York, in particular, once owned and cherished by black families and passed down, were often sold off by the grandkids, who were tempted by the extraordinary amount of money outsiders were willing to pay. So they took it, moved from the North and returned South almost as if they could somehow return to their roots — or at least the roots that they knew. Some would call it progress. She couldn't.

Connor wiped sweat from the back of his neck and loaded another pallet of wood onto the truck. They were making good progress on the interior foundations. One of his main concerns on projects like these was safety. The buildings were not just old, they'd been in disrepair for decades. He didn't want any ceilings or walls falling on his men. They had four more buildings to shore up and then the interior work could begin in earnest.

Jake caught up with him. "Hey, that Victor guy is up at the main building. Said he wanted to talk to you."

Connor's jaw tightened. "Did he say what he wanted?"

"No, just that he wanted to see you. Maybe it's about that job up in New York."

"No reason to get me involved. That's Olivia's decision." Over coffee, earlier that morning, Jake had poked and prodded Connor about how things were going with him and Olivia. He'd been stingy with details but offered up enough for Jake to know that he cared about her. He'd also told him about her job offer and her decision to take it, playing down his feelings about it.

Connor loaded the pallet on the back of the truck, took off his gloves and stuck them in his back pocket. Several things were running through his head about Victor's unannounced visit and he didn't like any of them. "Take this truck down to building twelve. The guys are waiting on this wood."

"Sure. Hey, you cool? You want me to come with you? I can send someone else with the truck."

"Naw. I'm good. He'll be safe with me," he said, half in jest, and began the short walk to the main building.

Victor was waiting out front, starched and

polished. Connor had never seen one individual look so out of place.

"Mr. Randall, what can I do for you today?" he asked as he walked up on Victor.

Victor lifted his chin and offered a mock smile. "I was hoping to get a moment of your time."

"I'm here. So take your moment." He folded his arms across his chest and planted his feet.

Victor cleared his throat. "Olivia informed me this morning that she wasn't going to take the position at The Institute."

Connor masked his surprise. "And you felt the need to tell me, because . . ."

"Olivia is extremely talented, brilliant, actually. This position will open a world of opportunity for her that I don't think she is taking into consideration." He lowered his gaze for a moment, then looked directly at Connor. "I was hoping that you would talk to her and help her to change her mind."

"What makes you think that I can change her mind?"

"I'm not a stupid man, Mr. Lawson."

They both understood what he meant.

"I may have put her off with . . . caveats that she . . . was unwilling to concede. Those are off the table." He cleared his throat again. "All I want is the best for

Olivia." He paused. "And I think you do, too." He extended his hand to Connor.

Connor stared at the olive branch for a moment and then extended his as well for a firm shake.

Victor gave a tight-lipped smile and a short nod of his head and walked off toward his car.

At that moment a light breeze could have knocked Connor over as he watched Victor walk away.

CHAPTER 14

Olivia arrived at the site in the late afternoon and went in search of Connor. One of the workers pointed her in the direction of the building at the far end of the property, the one where she'd found the folder. She grabbed a hard hat from the hook outside the door and went inside.

Several of the crew were inside, refitting the rafters of the shack. The spotlights were on, saws were buzzing, hammers were hammering. There were power wires and tools spread around the space and the hearty sound of men at work. Olivia spotted Connor at the back of the room, giving direction to the team that was hoisting the ceiling beam. She stood out of the way and waited until he was satisfied with the positioning. When he turned around the serious lines around his eyes and mouth softened when he saw her. A smile crept across his mouth. He walked toward her and his

Southern upbringing almost had him taking off his hat in the presence of a lady, but he remembered where he was and good sense prevailed.

"You made it." He walked up to her. "Kind of busy in here today."

"I see." She glanced up. "Great job. Looks just like the original."

"We try," he said with a grin. "Let's step outside." He led her out. "So what are you going to work on today?"

"I was hoping I might get lucky and uncover some other treasures." She smiled. "I'll be examining the old schoolhouse."

"The foundation and roof have been done on that building so you should be fine. I can send down one of the power lamps if you need it."

"That would be great. Thanks." She reached out and touched his arm, took a quick look around to make sure no one was watching, and said, "I told him no."

"I know," Connor said softly.

Olivia frowned. "What do you mean, you know?"

"Victor was here a couple of hours ago. He told me."

Olivia blinked in surprise. "He was here? Why in the world would he come here to tell you that?"

"He asked for my help. He wants me to convince you to take the job."

"*He* wants *you* to convince me? Why would he think that you would?"

"According to him, 'he's not a stupid man,' " Connor said, the innuendo clear.

Olivia flushed.

"What made you change your mind? This morning you said you would take it."

"The words flowed out of my mouth without me thinking about it and when I heard them I knew I'd made the right decision — for me."

He stepped closer. "You're sure?"

She nodded.

"Then, my job is done," he teased.

Olivia laughed. "Anyway, I should get to work."

"Listen, I was thinking that maybe we could do a dinner cruise tonight if you're up for it."

Her eyes brightened. "Sure."

"I'll call and make reservations. Seven good?"

"Perfect." *And Desiree said he didn't date.*

"I'll see you later." He leaned in and kissed her lightly on the lips.

"People will talk," she whispered.

"Let them."

Her heart leaped in her chest as he strolled

back inside.

"I'm going to have to start shopping for outfits if this keeps up," Olivia said to Desiree as they walked to the day spa that was located on The Port's premises.

"Told you that you were special."

Olivia's face warmed.

"How is your research coming?"

"Great!" She told Desiree about her find of the folder and her discoveries earlier in the day in the old schoolhouse. "There were some very worn notebooks with what looks like children's work. Most of the writing is faded but it all has value. Old desks and chairs, and I found an actual abacus."

"Wow. That's amazing. There is so much history here at the harbor. When I first moved out here to be with Lincoln, I had no idea the impact that African-Americans had on the area."

"I know. With this restoration and the ephemera that I'm finding, there's no telling what long-term effects it will have on the area."

"What do you mean?" Desiree opened the glass door that led to the spa.

"Once the homestead is fully restored, it will certainly get landmark status, the value of the surrounding community will go up and it will bring in tourists, which is a boon to the economy."

"Never thought of it that way, but you're right."

They stepped inside the spa. There were two other women waiting, reading magazines, swathed in thick white terry-cloth robes.

Layla stepped in from the back room. Her face lit up when she saw Desiree. "Hey, lady, how are you? Did you have an appointment?"

"No. But I wanted you to meet Olivia Gray."

"Nice to meet you. Are you visiting or are you new to town?"

"I'm here on a work assignment, actually. I'm working on the restoration research of the Dayton Village."

"Really? So is my cousin-in-law Connor. Have you met him?"

Olivia blushed. "Um, yes, we've met."

It took a moment for the inflection of the comment to register and when it did the surprise was evident. "Well, it's about time," she said.

Olivia blinked. "What do you mean?"

"You didn't get this from me, but I never liked Adrienne and cheered her departure from his life."

Adrienne? Connor had never mentioned her. "Oh."

There was an awkward pause. "I'm sorry. I . . ."

"Please. No worries," Olivia said, even as she wondered about Adrienne and what she meant to Connor.

Desiree lowered her voice so that the waiting women wouldn't hear. "I was hoping that you could squeeze Olivia in."

"I'll make it work. Can you wait about a half hour? I can take care of you myself."

"Sure. Thank you."

"I will leave you ladies to do your thing." Desiree squeezed Olivia's arm and walked out.

"Come on in the back and get changed," Layla said.

Olivia followed Layla down the hallway to the changing rooms.

"You can put your things in one of the lockers. Do you know what you want done?"

"Just a great massage, maybe a facial."

"Not a problem. Once you're done changing, you can take a shower and then you can go into room four. I'll be with you shortly. Can I get you anything? Tea, glass of wine?"

"Glass of wine sounds great."

Layla grinned. "I'll have one of my assistants bring it to the room. See you in a few."

Olivia got undressed and found her way to the shower, then got settled in room four. As promised, a glass of wine was waiting for her.

The room was dimly lit with soft lighting. A soothing scent that she couldn't quite place floated in the air and the sound of waterfalls rounded out the tranquil atmosphere.

Olivia relaxed on the chaise lounge and sipped her wine. She leaned her head back and tried to imagine what this Adrienne was like, what kind of relationship she'd had with Connor, for how long. Had they been in love? Or was it just a "thing"? How long ago had they parted ways?

She closed her eyes. Why did it matter? What was going on between them was temporary. They both knew that, which was what made her growing feelings for Connor Lawson hard to accept.

"Sorry, things took longer than I anticipated."

Olivia opened her eyes and sat up. "No problem. The atmosphere is perfect."

"Well, let's get you started. I'll step out and you can take off the robe and get settled on the table. Lie on your stomach."

"Okay."

Moments later Layla returned. "Any special places that need extra attention?"

"My shoulders and neck."

"Okay. Just relax." Layla set up her oils, poured some in her hands to warm them and began her work on Olivia. Her skilled fingers kneaded deep in the tight muscles of her neck. Olivia moaned in pleasure.

Olivia wanted to quiz Layla about Connor, but she was feeling so good and relaxed her mind had disconnected from her body. She felt herself floating away.

An hour later Layla whispered that she was done and that Olivia could get dressed. Olivia pulled herself up from the tender grasp of sleep.

"I feel amazing," she said.

"That's our motto. See you up front."

Olivia got dressed and went to the reception area. It was empty save for Layla.

"How much do I owe you?"

"It's on the house. Any woman who can catch my cousin's eye is all right in my book." She rested her arms on the counter. "He's really a good guy, you know."

"I think I do."

"Adrienne really did a number on him."

"How so?"

Layla glanced away. "I've said too much already. Connor should be the one to tell you if he wants you to know. But I will say this — treat him good. Okay? He deserves it."

"I believe that."

"Come by anytime. How long will you be in town?"

"At least another six weeks."

"Hope to see you again."

"You will."

CHAPTER 15

The atmosphere aboard the boat was the ultimate in romance. To add to the ambience, the perfect weather and smooth waters, the "cruise to nowhere" had booked the soul singer Ledisi to perform.

"Oh, my goodness. I love her!" Olivia enthused. "Did you know she was going to perform?" she asked as they were being shown to their table on the top deck.

"I had a hint."

Olivia playfully nudged Connor in the side.

"I'll be your server for the evening." The young woman who approached them seemed to be speaking more to Connor than to the two of them. Olivia bit back a smile. The waitress could look all she wanted, but he was going home with her. "Can I get you something to drink to start?"

Connor ordered a bourbon and Olivia a glass of wine.

"Be right back," the woman said, and sashayed away with an extra roll to her hips.

Connor seemed oblivious to her come-on and focused on the menu. "Food looks good."

The more she was with him the more Olivia was beginning to believe that she really was special. But as much as she wanted to simply let go and enjoy the ride, there was that part of her that hesitated. At some point the shoe would fall. It always did, and she would be wise to keep that at the forefront of her thoughts. No matter how wonderful Connor seemed, he was no different from all the others who'd come and gone in her life. She couldn't let good looks, great sex and heart-stopping charm allow her to forget what was real and what was fantasy.

The waitress returned shortly with their drinks and took their dinner orders.

"To a wonderful night," Connor said, raising his glass.

Olivia touched her glass to his.

Connor angled his head slightly to the side. "So . . . how long were you and Victor together?"

Olivia bristled. "Why does that matter?"

"It just seemed that he's overly involved in your life. That's usually because there's still something there."

Olivia set her drink down. "I can't speak for Victor. I can only speak for myself, and beside the fact that we are on two opposite ends of the spectrum, Victor wants something that I can't give him."

Connor stared at her above the rim of his glass. "What is that?"

"Permanence. A future. Even if I had feelings for him, which I don't, I can't see myself tied down to anyone."

Connor was thoughtful. He wasn't sure how he felt about what she'd said. He should feel some sense of relief. But he didn't.

"Totally understandable," he finally said. He tossed back the rest of his drink. "With the kind of work that you do, it would be hard to maintain any kind of meaningful relationship."

Olivia inwardly flinched. "Exactly."

"I feel the same way."

"Oh. Makes sense," she said, in a barely audible voice.

The waitress arrived with their meals and the tight line of tension that was lengthening between them was momentarily broken.

Dinner and the entertainment were both excellent and put them back in a good mood. By the time they disembarked from the boat they were literally on solid ground, the comments of earlier at least pushed aside if not forgotten.

"Want to join me for a run in the morning?" Connor asked as he slid his arm around her waist.

It was a loaded question and they both knew it.

"Mind if I take a rain check?"

His mouth tightened ever so slightly. "Sure." He pulled his cell phone from his pocket and checked the time. "Getting late. Let me take you home."

Why was she disappointed? "Sure."

"Thank you for tonight," Olivia said when they pulled to a stop in front of her cottage.

"I enjoyed myself." He got out of the car, came around and opened her door. "Get some rest," he said, and lightly kissed her forehead.

Before Olivia could react he'd turned and gotten back in the car. She spun away and tried to fight off the tightness that was building in her throat. She'd never gotten a chance to talk to him about Adrienne. Maybe it was just as well.

In bed that night, alone, she tried to piece

together what was happening between her and Connor. Clearly there was an attraction. Was it totally sexual? That was the vibe she'd gotten from him when she'd declined to run with him in the morning. She knew what he was asking. He wanted them to spend the night together, and when she said no to him, his whole attitude toward her changed. Maybe all he wanted was sex. So what? That was all she wanted. Then, why did she feel so crappy?

Connor was in a foul mood when he arrived at the work site. Everything and everyone seemed to piss him off. He spent all morning barking orders and slamming things around, yelling at the crew for any and everything.

"Maybe you should go home," Jake said, coming up behind him.

Connor glanced over his shoulder. "What the hell are you talking about? There's work to be done and I'm working with a bunch of idiots," he grumbled, and tossed a bag of tools into the back of the truck.

"If you're suddenly working with a bunch of idiots, that says more about you than it does about them."

Connor spun around, his expression a storm cloud waiting to erupt. "What the hell are you talking about?"

"I'm saying you hired these 'idiots' and if you don't get the bug out of your ass you're going to be the only idiot left on the job," he said from between his teeth.

Connor's jaw clenched.

"What is wrong with you today?"

"Nothing."

"Let me try again. What's wrong with you? Is it Olivia?"

Connor's brow tightened. "No."

"Wrong answer." Jake waited a beat. "Something happen?"

"No."

"You want to talk?"

"Nothing to talk about."

"Cool. I'm going to the office. I need to call the vendor."

Connor grumbled something under his breath. He knew Jake was right. He felt raw inside, as if a scab had been ripped off before whatever was underneath had healed. Not getting more than an hour's sleep didn't help his mood, either. He leaned against the side of the truck and looked around. His men were excellent workers and he knew it. He lowered his head and then started off toward the office.

Jake was hanging up the phone when Connor walked in.

"Think I'll take your advice and head home. Didn't sleep well last night."

"Hmm."

"Went on one of those dinner cruises."

"Yeah?" he said, noncommittal. He organized some papers on the desk. "Went with Olivia?"

"Yeah."

"Guess that's why you didn't get any sleep," Jake said with an inquiring lift of his eyes.

"Something like that. Dropped her off and I went home."

"She decide what she's going to do about the job offer?"

"Not going to take it."

"Really? Humph. Is that a good thing?"

"Yeah, I suppose."

"She coming out here today?"

"Not sure."

"Maybe you should find out."

The two men looked at each other, the understanding of longtime friendship in their eyes.

"Yeah, I probably should."

"I can handle things from here."

"Thanks." Connor turned to go, stopped and looked back. "Thanks."

Jake waved him off and returned to the task at hand.

■ ■ ■ ■

Olivia finished writing up her report, reviewed it one more time and hit Send. The leather folder and the two class books that she was able to salvage were sealed in plastic and she'd placed them in a special glass container that she'd brought along specifically for something like this.

She stared at the items through the glass. In there was life — adventures and memories of those long gone. They'd left a trail of clues about their existence, something to say, "Yes, I was here." Like teens did when they carved their names in trees or painted them on walls. She smiled. Everyone wanted to let the world know that they existed and that they would be remembered when they were gone. Who would remember her? Even her last foster parents were gone, having passed away years earlier. That pit began to open in her stomach again and if she didn't snap out of it, she'd be sucked in.

She shook her head to try to dispel the melancholy, and had begun to gather the things that were spread out on the table when the doorbell rang. She checked the time. It was barely ten o'clock. Desiree said she might stop by but this was early even for her. Olivia got up and went to the door.

"Connor." Her stomach jumped and sent her heart racing.

"Mornin'." He took her in with a sweeping glance. "I should have called first."

"It's not a problem. Do you want to come in?"

"Thanks."

The heat of him touched her as he passed and her eyes fluttered closed for an instant. She shut the door and followed him inside.

"Can I get you anything? Have you had breakfast?"

He turned to her and grinned and her insides lit up.

"I ate about four hours ago. But I'd love some coffee if you have it."

"Sure. Come on in the kitchen." She took out the package of coffee filters, discarded the old one and prepared a fresh batch. "So how is everything going at the work site?" She took a seat at the counter.

"I was kicked off the project today."

"What!"

The corner of his mouth curved into a grin. He held up his hand. "Not officially. Jake told me to get lost. Said I had a bad attitude."

Olivia's thoughts settled down. "Oh." She pressed her hand to her chest. "And why would he say that?"

"He thinks it might have something to do with you."

"Me?" She frowned.

Connor pushed out a breath and pressed his palms onto the countertop. "Look, I don't do this whole relationship thing. It's been a long time . . . and with good reason. So I don't know what will happen between me and you. Maybe something, maybe nothing at all. Once we're finished with this project —" he gave a slight shrug "— who knows. But there are no guarantees, not from me. And before we take this any further, I need to be sure that we're both in the same place about this."

Olivia didn't know if she was hurt or relieved. On the one hand he was pretty much telling her that he wasn't going to commit and that this was purely sexual. And at the same time he held out the carrot of hope that "maybe" things "might" work between them. But wasn't that what she wanted — a friend with benefits? Besides, how could she ever commit and be fully true to anyone, share a life with anyone, when she didn't really know who she was?

"You're absolutely right. Neither one of us is in a position to focus on anything beyond right here and now. We both have so much going on. Let's just enjoy the time we have together and leave it at that."

A glint of surprise registered in his eyes and then was gone. He nodded in agreement.

Olivia jumped up from her seat and spun away before he saw the shimmer of tears that suddenly sprang up in her eyes. She took out two mugs from the cabinet and filled them.

She and Connor sealed their tacit agreement over coffee and talked about other things, impersonal things, not the things that were really weighing down their souls. It was better that way.

"Thanks for the coffee and the conversation." He stood in the front doorway. "There's an art exhibit opening tonight at the Grenning Gallery. Think you might want to go?"

"Oh, I think I saw a flyer for that when I was in town." She held the door open. "Sure. That sounds good. I can meet you there."

His eyes flashed for a second. "Okay. It opens at seven. Maybe we can do dinner after."

"Perfect."

He turned to leave. "If you change your

mind and want me to pick you up, let me know."

"Okay."

He jogged down the two steps of the front porch and strode off toward his truck. Olivia didn't wait for him to pull off before she went inside and shut the door.

"I don't understand why you're upset," Desiree was saying. "This is the way you wanted things, easy with no strings." She took a forkful of tossed salad.

"I know that's what I said." Olivia slowly spun her glass of iced green tea in a circle on the table.

"But . . ."

"But I didn't think that I would start to care for him."

"It would be hard not to fall for a man like Connor Lawson."

"So now what?"

Desiree blew out a breath. "You either put your cards on the table and be honest with him or you let things go the way they've been going."

"I'm *not* going to tell him how I feel," she insisted with a vigorous shake of her head. "He made it pretty clear where he stood."

"Then, there is always option number three."

"What's that?"

"Get out before someone gets hurt," her friend said with soft conviction.

CHAPTER 16

Olivia found a parking space around the corner from the gallery, then walked back to the front entrance. She stood to the side to let the patrons enter while she looked for Connor. It was a bit after seven. She stood there for another ten minutes, beginning to feel silly and maybe stood up, when she spotted him strolling down the street. Relief and that rush that she always felt when she saw him rapidly filled her.

"Hi." He leaned in and kissed her cheek. She inhaled him. "Sorry to make you wait. I decided to leave my car at home, since you were driving. I walked over. A bit longer than I remember," he added with a smile.

"It's fine. Really." Her eyes moved over his face and she so wanted to be held by him, right there in the middle of the street. "So I'm the designated driver for the night."

He grinned and the sun rose in the middle of the evening.

"You can handle it." He placed his hand firmly at the small of her back and guided her inside.

The two-story gallery was one of the cultural centerpieces of the town. It was known to host author book signings, concerts, and fund-raising events. There was always something special set up around the holidays and, of course, art exhibits — from the famous to the budding artist. Tonight's pieces were by a young artist who was starting to make a name for himself with his eclectic blend of abstract and three-dimensional art.

Olivia and Connor strolled around, looking at and commenting on the pieces, often having the very same likes and dislikes. They'd stopped at the buffet table and were selecting a couple of the canapés when Connor's name was called. They both turned.

Olivia felt the muscles in Connor's arm tighten.

"Adrienne."

She walked up to him as if Olivia was invisible, and kissed him. "Good to see you."

"Surprised to see you." His jaw clenched as he wiped his lips with the pad of his thumb. He took Olivia's hand. "Adrienne Forde, Dr. Olivia Gray."

Adrienne turned her green eyes on Olivia.

Her finely arched right brow rose. "What kind of doctor?"

So *this* was the infamous Adrienne. "Anthropology."

"Must be nice." The woman refocused her attention on Connor. "I'll be in town for a few days doing some research. I'm pitching a television special. I'll give you a call. Nice to meet you, Doctor." She turned and was quickly swallowed up in the crowd.

Connor's body vibrated like a tapped tuning fork. The mere mention of a television show, combined with running into Adrienne, was enough to ruin a perfectly wonderful evening. A shadow settled on his face, clouded his eyes and somehow obscured his features.

"Let's get out of here." His grip tightened on Olivia's hand as he led her to the exit and out. "Where are you parked?"

"Around the corner."

"Come on. We'll find someplace to have dinner, or you can just drop me home if you want. Up to you."

She tugged on his hand to stop his forward stride. "You want to tell me what the hell that was back there and what's going on now?"

"No."

Her eyes widened in shock. "Fine. I'm not

really hungry anyway. Why don't I just drop you off?"

"That's probably best."

She breezed by him, forcing him to lengthen his stride to catch up with her. He caught her by the arm and spun her around.

"I don't want to talk about it. Okay? Not now." He frowned. "Maybe some other time."

"Fine. Whatever, Connor." She snatched her arm out of his grip.

"So it's okay for your former lover to come to me to try to get you to do what he wants, so he can get in your pants, but I can't get a friendly kiss without you getting pissed?"

Olivia whirled around so fast her head spun. "What! Are you out of your freaking mind? Did you really say that to me?" She was up in his face. The fury racing through her veins blinded her to everything around them.

"Forget it. I'll walk." He turned away as a maelstrom of emotions raced through his head. He knew what he felt and what he really wanted to say, but he couldn't. He simply could not.

"So this is how it's going to be," she said softly, halting him in midstride.

He turned around, his head slightly lowered, and then he looked at her and knew in an instant how crazy he was acting. Suddenly, the hurt that had taken the sparkle out of her eyes mirrored his own. He'd done that.

Connor blew out a breath from between parted lips. He slid his hands into his pockets and came toward her. Her eyes glistened and she blinked rapidly. His stomach twisted.

"I'm sorry. You didn't deserve whatever the hell that was that I just pulled."

Olivia pressed her trembling lips tightly together.

Connor reached out and cupped her cheek in his palm. "I'm sorry," he whispered.

Olivia swallowed over the tight knot in her throat. "You still feel like walking home?"

"Are you coming inside?" Connor asked when they pulled up in front of his house. "The least I can do is whip us up something to eat. I'm starved. And you don't even have to go running with me in the morning."

Her insides softened. She knew what he meant and she appreciated him all the more for it. "I am pretty starved myself. What can you make beside jambalaya?"

"Dr. Gray, my skills are limitless." He

opened the car door, got out and came around to help her out.

"You relax, put on the television or some music, whatever you want. I'm going to see what's in the fridge."

"Sure you don't need any help?"

"Nope. Want some wine or something stronger?"

"Hmm, maybe I'll try a bourbon."

His entire expression registered surprise. "Coming right up." He fixed her a small shot with ice and brought it to her. "It has a kick to it."

"I can handle myself." She took the shot glass. "Thank you."

Connor eyed her for a moment, then went into the kitchen.

Olivia lifted the glass to her nose and inhaled, then took her first sip. The liquor burst with heat and flavor on her tongue, then lit tiny fires down her throat and seared through her veins, awakening her, bringing her to full attention, then rocking her into a sense of ease.

"Wow." *No wonder this is his drink of choice.*

Connor remembered he had a nice-size piece of salmon that he could season and grill, some baby potatoes and sautéed zucchini. He was at work preparing dinner when Olivia joined him in the kitchen.

"Refill?" he asked, briefly looking up from his preparations.

Olivia hopped up on the bar stool. "Oh, no. Not yet."

He grinned.

"What's on the menu?"

"Grilled salmon, seasoned to perfection, I might add, and sautéed zucchini with baby potatoes."

"Yum."

"I have some sorbet in the freezer for later if you want."

"Double yum." She put her glass down. "Are you sure I can't help with anything?"

"Positive."

They were quiet for a moment. "We are making a lot of progress on the site," Connor finally said. "We have about three more structures that need foundation work and then the real restoration can begin."

"You'll be working from sketches and photographs?"

"Yes, pretty much, as well as using what's left and restoring as much as possible to its original condition."

"I'd really like to be involved in the process. I'm sure I can help."

"I was thinking the same thing."

Their eyes met for an instant.

"Anything new with the items that you found the other day?"

"I sent all my notes and photos up to The Institute this morning. The items that I've collected so far are sealed and put away. I'm still blown away that the original freedom papers and birth certificates of the Dayton family were found intact."

They talked for a while about the long-term implications of what she'd found and how it would add to her credibility in the field.

"Not to mention what the finished product will mean for yours," Olivia said.

Connor put the plates on the table and then took the salmon out of the broiler and brought it to the table. He spooned the sautéed vegetables into a bowl.

"It's buffet so help yourself. How about a refill on your drink?"

She waved his offer away. "I'm good."

He chuckled and refilled his glass. "Wine?"

"That will work. Yes. Thanks."

He went to retrieve a bottle of wine from the living room wine cabinet and poured her a glass.

"To new beginnings," he said.

"And a lifetime of discoveries." She tapped her glass to his.

"You really are a Renaissance man," Olivia said after dinner. "You cook, you're handy with tools, you like art, music." *You're an incredible lover.*

Connor settled back on the couch. "I work hard at the things I enjoy." He reached for his glass and took a swallow.

"What's next for you after this project is completed?"

"Hmm, I was thinking about a short vacation, maybe to one of the islands, to just relax and unwind for a while. What about you?"

"Well, now that I won't be running things from behind a desk, I know that I want to go to South America and research some of the ruins. But that will be a while from now. Dayton Village is going to take up a great deal of time even after the work here is done. That's when mine really begins. There will be scholarly journals to write for, archival reports, speaking engagements, more papers to write." She smiled. "And I teach in the fall at Columbia."

"Oh, really? I didn't know that."

"Yes, I've been there about five years now. I love it."

"You're a busy lady."

All she had was her work.

"So the only time you get to play and relax is while you're working."

"Hmm, pretty much."

"When was the last time you were on a real vacation, one that had nothing to do with work?"

She thought for a moment. "Wow, I . . . don't remember."

"All work and no play . . ."

"My work is who I am, what I do," she countered.

"That is so far from the truth. You use work to identify yourself, to make you whole." He moved closer to her on the couch. "You're so much more than that." He stared into her eyes until she looked away.

"You have no idea who I am . . . and neither do I."

"Olivia, I can't say that I can imagine or understand what it's like not to know your birth parents, but that's only a toss of the dice and genetics. The result of it all is you. You're the woman you are because you decided it was who you wanted to be." He was thoughtful for a moment. "When we met I was good with the whole idea that whatever happened between us was temporary. We'd enjoy each other for the time being and move on. That's the way I'd been living my life, no matter what it was that the woman wanted. So it was easy for me to walk away when it was over for me, because I was the only person that mattered. And everyone knew the rules going in." He shifted his position. "But you aren't all agreeable to this temporary thing because you don't want to get involved. You're afraid of giving yourself fully to anyone."

Olivia turned her face away. "That's not true."

"Of course it is." He pushed out a breath. "Adrienne is my reason. Fear is yours."

Olivia slowly turned her head. "What did she do?"

He looked off into the distance, seeing the past come to life. "We'd been seeing each other exclusively for about a year. She's an art buyer for several galleries around the country. That's how we met. She was building her brand and there was even talk about having her open her own gallery with one-of-a-kind pieces from around the world. That takes money, of course. Anyway, I knew I wasn't ready to settle down. I was establishing myself in my business, making a name, enjoying life. And then one day she tells me that she's pregnant. If there was one thing that was grilled into us Lawsons from the time we could understand, it was that we were to be honorable men. So, as an honorable man, I did the honorable thing and asked her to marry me. Bought her the biggest diamond I could find, took her home to meet the family, and a week before the very quickly put together wedding, I walked in on a conversation that she was having with her best friend, Claire." He snorted a derisive laugh. "Apparently the whole pregnancy was a ruse, and if she really was pregnant she wasn't sure if it was mine or Jeremy Blake's, her supposed-to-be ex's. She thought that was quite funny. My lucky number was drawn because I had the name and the money to help her finance her dream."

Olivia mumbled a curse under her breath. She could still see the hurt behind his eyes.

"The thing was I cared about Adrienne. I would have made a go of it." Connor swallowed. "After that . . ." He shrugged, then finished off his drink.

Olivia sadly shook her head. In her wildest dreams she couldn't imagine any woman not wanting this man in all the right ways. The pickings were slim when it came to truly eligible men. But it was women like Adrienne Forde that made it bad for everyone else.

"I take it she wants you back."

"So she says. She's been saying that in one way or the other for the past couple of years."

"And?"

"And what?"

"Does she have a chance at getting you back?" Olivia asked, as casually as she could.

"*Your* job is uncovering and returning to the past. Not mine."

"You restore and repair what's found, worn and broken," she said softly.

He reached out and caressed her cheek. "I try, Olivia. But I can't with you if you won't let me."

For an instant her heart stopped. "I . . . I didn't know that you wanted to try."

"Now you do." He pulled her into his arms and covered her mouth with his.

CHAPTER 17

In the following weeks Olivia and Connor spent most of their free time together, taking in the sights of the town, talking, sharing the highlights of their workday and slowly allowing some of their walls to come down.

For Olivia it was more difficult. Connor had to deal with only a single altering event in his life. It hadn't shaped him; it had merely shifted his direction. She had to face the idea that what ate at her soul was decades in the making and she might never be whole, at least not in the way that Connor needed and deserved. But she kept those thoughts to herself and tried as best she could to believe that this thing between them could ever be more than temporary.

Connor had to go into town to pick up a shipment of supplies that had arrived. While he loaded his truck, Ruth Farmer, a retired local librarian, stopped to chat and ask about the progress of the restoration.

"Things are coming along slowly but surely, Ms. Farmer. Several of the buildings are completed. I give it another two months and we should be done."

"That is just wonderful. I was so sad to see that no one ever took an interest in the place. There is so much of our history on that land."

"Very true."

Suddenly her dim blue-gray eyes sparkled with life. "Did you know that about fifteen years ago the library served as the local Chamber of Commerce?"

"No, I didn't know that."

"But there was a terrible fire. So much was destroyed," she said sadly. "But —" she raised a thin finger "— I was able to salvage some of the books. They weren't in any condition to return to the new library, so I kept them stored away in my attic. I'm almost positive I have something in there on Dayton Village."

"Would you mind if I take a look? I'm working with Dr. Gray from New York. She's doing the research on the original settlers. I'm sure she would be interested in whatever you might have."

"Of course. Of course. Do you want to

come now?"

He thought about the supplies that were needed back at the site. "Sure. That would be great. I'll just take a quick look."

He followed her home and she took him up to the attic, where there were at least two dozen boxes filled with the remains of the library collection.

Ms. Farmer gingerly walked around the boxes toward the back wall. "I tried to label them as best as I could. It's the librarian in me," she said with a grin. "The box that should have the Dayton Village memorabilia should be back here." She pushed aside a naked mannequin and stepped around an old wooden chest that looked as if it should have been on a pirate's ship. "Yes! Here it is." She stepped aside. "The one on top."

Connor walked around her and lifted the box down from the top of the stack and set it on the floor. Dust blew into his face. He brushed a coating of it off the top of the box with his work glove and took off the lid.

"You take all the time you need." She patted his shoulder and left him to work.

Connor sat on the floor and lifted the contents out of the box. Carefully, one by one, he went through the papers and books, many of them too distorted and damaged by age, fire and water to be of much use, at least not to him. But then he stopped cold when opened a book and saw a grainy sepia photograph of a woman who could have easily been Olivia's twin seventy-five years earlier. Her name was Ellen Dayton and it was her wedding photo to Robert Holmes. The next page told of Ellen and Robert's daughter Constance, who married Phillip Gray and had a daughter with him, Leslie Gray. The images were too distorted to make out. There was no indication that Leslie had ever married, only that she'd gone away to school to Atlanta, at Spelman. *The same city where Olivia grew up.* The pages after that were too badly damaged to make out.

Connor's pulse raced. He knew he had something. He could feel it. What it all meant he wasn't sure. He asked Ms. Farmer if he could borrow the book, with the promise that he would take excellent care of it and return it to her.

He made a quick stop at the site, unloaded the truck and told Jake that he would be gone for the rest of the day. He called Olivia. She was still on the road from her day trip to Manhattan. She said she should be back in town in about an hour or more.

"Can you meet me at my house?"

She talked to him through her headphones. "Sure. Is everything okay?"

"Yes. See you when you get here."

Connor kept staring at the photograph of Ellen Dayton. The resemblance was uncanny, right down to the tiny cleft in her chin. Cleft chins were a genetic trait passed down from parent to child. What if Olivia *was* a descendent and this wasn't some fluke discovery? Maybe she still had family out there, a real family. And if she did, maybe then she could get the answers that she'd been spending her life searching for.

How could anyone have given her up, given her away? They had no idea of the incredible woman that she would become, despite them.

Olivia was amazing. She was brilliant and kind and sexy and loving. Had he been looking for a woman, he would have been looking for an Olivia Gray. But he wasn't looking and that was precisely why she was in his life. She was supposed to be. He could try to downplay it and not feed into what had happened between them over the past couple of months. But despite the roadblocks and the temporary walls, he had fallen in love with her.

The reality hit him like a punch in the gut.

It stole his breath and for a moment his thoughts swam and struggled to rise to the surface. *He was in love with her.* "I'm in love with her." Saying the words out loud gave them life.

Connor pushed up from the couch and slowly paced the room. Loving her would never be enough. If he knew nothing else about Olivia, he knew that she was not willing and was unable to truly give in to love with anyone until she understood and found out who she was.

He glanced over his shoulder to the worn book on the table. In those pages and somewhere out there might be the answers that she was looking for. But what if they weren't? What if it was all an awful coincidence, and he was the one that would give her hope when there wasn't any? Could he do that to her?

His ringing phone interrupted the turn of his thoughts. He snatched it up from the table and a half smile lifted his mouth.

"Hey, sis."

"Hey, big brother. Long time. How are you? You don't call, you don't write," she teased.

Connor chuckled. "Very funny. I could say the same thing about you, Sydni. You don't stay still long enough to call or write. So to what do I owe the pleasure?" He plopped down on the couch and stretched out his long legs.

"Well, if you must know, I'm pregnant!"

"What! Congratulations, sis. How is Gabriel taking it?"

"He is beyond thrilled," she said, the joy in her voice palpable.

"I guess this means traveling the world is going to have to slow down for a bit."

"Yes, but I'm fine with that."

"You?" He chuckled. His sister was the next in charge of their father's mega global marketing enterprise. They handled some of the biggest corporations and überentertainers and executives in the country and out, which was how she'd met her husband, Gabriel St. James. Connor was hard-pressed to see his sister puttering around in their sprawling house cooing and burping a baby. But anything was possible.

"Anyway, the reason why I'm calling is, of course, to share my news with my big brother. But I — we, Gabe and I — want you to be our child's godfather."

For the second time in less than an hour the wind was knocked out of him. "Sis, are you sure? I mean, of course I will."

"Thank you, CJ," she said. It was her pet name for him since they were kids — Connor James. "I know it all seems kind of soon, but you know me, plan ahead." She laughed.

"How far along?"

"Four months."

"And you're just getting around to telling me?"

"We wanted to wait, make sure everything was okay."

"Hmm, I get it. And . . . is everything okay?"

"So far." She paused. "The doctor says that I have a few medical issues and I will probably be on bed rest in my last few months. But we will have to see."

His body tensed. "What kind of medical issues?"

"Apparently I have a weak cervix, and a heart murmur, which supposedly I've had since I was a child. But no one ever told me."

He snapped his head at the news. "Are you okay? That's all I want to know."

"Yes, yes, I'm fine. I'm taking it easy, taking my vitamins and doing what the doctor says. So please don't worry."

"Too late on that score." Connor leaned forward and rested his arms on his thighs. "Does Dad know?"

"Not yet. I was planning to tell him over the weekend. I'm going to have to stop working in about another month or two. That's going to send shock waves through the company."

"They'll survive. The important thing is you and your baby."

"My sentiments exactly! So enough about me. What's going on with you? How is the project going? What's happening in your life?"

Connor leaned back, his body slowly relaxing. "Well . . ."

"Oh, CJ, I am beyond happy for you. You have no idea. After that witch Adrienne . . . Grrr. Every time I think about her I want to catch her after work and give her a Nawlins beat down."

Connor broke out laughing.

"I'm serious."

"She was here."

"Say what?"

"Adrienne was here a few weeks back. Still trying to get me to forgive her and start over."

"You have got to be kidding. The nerve. She knows she blew a good thing. Anyway, I don't want to talk about her. I want to meet Olivia. I have to meet her. Any woman who can put that kind of soft bass in your voice has to be my kind of girl," she teased.

Connor chuckled. "In due time." He hesitated, unsure of how much he should reveal to his sister. But growing up, he and Sydni had been thick as thieves, covering for each other, sticking up for each other, sharing their adventures, getting advice. If anyone would understand, Sydni would. "It's not quite as simple as it seems . . ."

"Damn, CJ, can't life ever be easy? Wow. Well, if you're asking for my advice I say tell her. Let her make the decision on whether or not she wants to pursue it. Because if she finds out later that you knew, and from everything you've told me about her she will, she will never forgive you. I know I wouldn't."

"You're probably right."

"Probably? I'm always right."

"No, you're not, Syd. We got that split down the middle."

"Hmm. If you say so. Anyway, do the right thing. Or at least what your soul tells you to do. And make plans to visit. I need to see you."

"I will. Listen, tell Gabe congrats, and you — you take care of yourself and my godchild."

She laughed. "I will. I have my feet up as we speak."

"Good girl."
"Love you, CJ," she said softly.
"Back at you."
The call ended and he put the phone down on the table next to the book.

CHAPTER 18

Olivia's nerves were still on edge from her confrontation with Victor. Never in her wildest dreams would she have thought that he would be so petty and stoop so low. Her fingers gripped the wheel. All her hard work, her years of dedication out the window, her research questioned. Unreal. He'd actually said out loud in front of staff members, at the meeting, that most of her time had been spent cultivating a relationship rather than doing her job. She was so stunned by what he'd said that for several moments she couldn't respond. Everyone in the room looked everywhere but at her. If that wasn't bad enough, he went on to insinuate that her research was questionable because the chain of custody was unclear. This was potentially one of the greatest discoveries of her career and Victor was determined to taint it in whatever way he could, simply because he couldn't have her the way he wanted.

She sniffed back the threat of tears. She refused to be broken by Victor Randall or anyone else. She was highly respected in her field and there would be plenty of opportunities out there for her. Besides, maybe it was time that she took a break, had a real vacation as Connor suggested.

Olivia turned on her headlights. She'd hoped to get back to Sag Harbor before it got dark. She was still a bit unfamiliar with the roads and the turns, and preferred to do her driving during the day. So much for that plan. Her exit was a mile up ahead. After that she had about another twenty-minute drive.

The closer she came, the more she realized how much she needed to see Connor. He had a way of soothing the ragged parts of her, filling up some of the empty spaces. And it wasn't so much what he did or said, it was his presence, just being there.

Many evenings they spent together doing nothing more than watching a movie or stretching out on the couch to listen to music. There wasn't always heavy discussion, or even light conversation. Some nights they were content simply being together in the same space. She'd never had that with a man before, being that kind of comfortable.

But tonight she needed to talk. She needed to pour out her frustration and her anger without censure. And then she needed to be held and to be told that it was Victor's loss, and that the best was right in front of her. She needed to be made love to and caressed and soothed, everything to make this day disappear.

Finally she pulled into town, thought about making a quick stop at the market, but didn't want to spend any more time away from Connor. She made the turn onto the single-lane road that led to his house.

"I asked you not to call me, Adrienne. We have nothing to talk about. Period."

"Connor, if we could just sit down, have drinks and talk . . . That's all I'm asking."

"You don't get it. There is nothing for us to talk about. We said it all."

"It's because of her, isn't it, the woman I saw you with?" she demanded, her tone shifting from pleading to accusatory.

"Whether or not that's true, it's none of your damned business."

"Then, it is true." She sniffed. "She's some big-time researcher at The Institute in New York. I looked her up."

Connor's chest tightened. The idea that

Adrienne was checking into Olivia didn't sit well with him at all.

"What is it about her? What can she do for you that I can't if you'd let me?"

"Adrienne, if whatever you thought you could do for me was lined with platinum, it wouldn't matter. What you did, to me, to us, can never be repaired. You lied and you swept dozens of others up in your lie."

"I know. Connor, please. I only did it because I was scared of losing you."

"I've heard it all before, Adrienne. You weren't scared of losing me. You were scared that you might lose your ticket to your well-orchestrated future. Look, I would hate to have to change my number. A great deal of my business is tied to this number. But I will do it to keep you from calling." He heard a car pull into the driveway. "Good-bye, Adrienne."

Adrienne looked out her car window and watched Olivia walk up to the house. Moments later the door opened and Connor greeted her with a sensual kiss. Adrienne waited for Olivia to go inside before she turned on her lights and drove away.

"How was the drive?" Connor draped his arm across Olivia's shoulder as they walked inside.

"Not bad." She rested her head on his shoulder.

"What's wrong?" He turned her to face him. His eyes scanned her face but her gaze wouldn't meet his. "Liv, what happened?"

Her throat clenched. She shook her head. "I don't know where to begin."

"Wherever you want to, just tell me what's going on?"

She walked over to the couch and sat.

"You want something to drink? Wine?"

"A little bourbon," she said with a weak smile, to his surprise.

"Not a problem." He fixed a drink for them both and brought them over. He sat next to her. "Tell me."

By the time Olivia finished retelling the unbelievable afternoon she'd had, Connor was beyond livid. Clearly Victor's "friendly" visit had been a bunch of bull and he'd only spouted a load of crap. His showboating at the meeting only added to the fury Connor was barely keeping a lid on after the call from Adrienne. It was one thing for Adrienne to do her number on him, but he would not stand idly by while that so-called man tried to eviscerate Olivia and all that she stood for. The more she explained and the more he heard the hurt and anger in her voice, the more determined he was to put an end to the BS once and for all.

"So where do you stand now with your job?"

"I still have a job, at least until my contract expires, but my credibility has been called into question with my colleagues, many of whom I supervise at one point or another." She snuggled closer and sipped her drink. The warm liquid softened the tattered fringes of her day, and allowed her to see it through a soft haze.

"In another month Victor will be gone. You still have work here to do, and the people that know you and know your reputation are not going to swallow that crap that he tried to shove down their throats. And if they do, then they were never in your corner or had your back. You do what you do best — research and evaluation. This project is major and you're taking the lead on it. Don't let Victor Randall rob you of that out of his own petty ego issues. Don't let today trip you up and make you lose focus or question yourself. I'm not going to let you do it, so don't even think about it."

She tilted her face up to him and smiled through watery eyes. "I know you're right. I told myself the same thing on the drive back. I guess what makes it so much harder is that Victor knows about some of my struggles with my identity and my roots, and it's because of those things that I work so hard on providing proof, being accurate, validating everything as if that somehow says that I'm good, I'm okay, I'm real. He used what he knew about me to try to hurt me." She snorted a laugh. "It's why I keep the walls up. Today was a result of what happens when you let someone in." She started to get up but her head spun, the bourbon hitting the spot, especially on an empty stomach.

Connor held her arm. "Are you saying that includes me?"

She looked at him but couldn't keep him in focus. "Only time will tell." She sighed heavily, unaware of how her remark stung him. She curled closer to him, rested her head on his chest and closed her eyes.

Connor leaned his head back against the couch and stretched his arm along Olivia's body. He would prove to her that what she would have with him could never be compared to what she'd experienced before. He'd be there for her no matter what the outcome was from the book that he'd found, or whatever happened with her job. They'd deal with it together.

He glanced down at her lightly sleeping form and eased out from under her. She needed food, a hot bath and then whatever happened between the sheets. Tomorrow he would tell her about the book.

Olivia blinked against the soft light that inched across the floor. She squinted at the bedside clock. It was nearly six thirty. She groaned softly and turned, delighted to find Connor still in bed and not halfway down the beach. Her eyes drifted close. By degrees the previous evening replayed in her head. She'd been an emotional mess when she'd arrived and had blurted and blubbered what had happened, all the while sipping on a glass of bourbon that had apparently gone straight to her head. The rest of the evening was a bit of a blur. She vaguely remembered eating and then being . . . bathed! Her eyes flew open and her body came fully alive.

She turned on her side to face Connor, who as always was gorgeously naked beneath the sheet. His arm was tossed across his eyes. Olivia grinned and gently lifted the sheet before sliding her body across his.

Connor groaned.

"Mornin'," she whispered as she slowly stroked him to life. "How about a little run around the bed to get the day started?" She buzzed in his ear before nibbling the lobe.

He clapped her rear end in his palms and

gently squeezed. "Be careful what you wish for, little lady," he said, his voice still rough with sleep. "Why don't you climb aboard and let's see what you got."

"My pleasure . . . or should I say ours." She straddled him and rested her weight on her knees while she positioned herself above his erection, which was clearly calling her name. The swollen head pressed against the slickness of her opening. She eased down and the first inch of him spread her, excited her. She bit down on her lip to keep from waking the neighbors as he filled her, until the air lodged in her lungs.

They found their rhythm and it flowed like hot lava coursing through their veins. The musical notes of their groans and sighs matched the tempo of their slow grind, which escalated to quick, hard thrusts and long undulations of hips.

Connor wanted to be everywhere at once: inside her, kissing her, suckling her, caressing her. It was maddening to want someone as much as he wanted her, and to want to satisfy her, put his mark on her so that she would never forget the magic that they made together. He would never get enough of her. Never.

Her entire body was one electrified nerve, sensitive to every touch, kiss, groan and whisper of her name, which all sent her closer and closer to the cliff of no return.

"Liv . . ." he moaned, pushing up hard inside her.

Her spine curved back, the veins in her neck pulsed, the tips of her nipples rose, the shudder began deep in her soul and like a lid lifted off a boiling pot of soup, she bubbled over. Connor grabbed her hips, holding her in place even as her insides sucked and quickened around him. He was on the brink. The tendons in his neck strained; his muscles tensed. The throb began deep in his loins, tightened, pulsed and expelled in one long upward thrust.

Olivia collapsed on his chest. Wave after wave of aftershock pleasure rolled through her. She was weak, spent and could easily while away the rest of her day holding Connor between her legs and listening to his heart beat against her ear. She closed her eyes and gave in to the moment.

Connor was still hard. He wanted her again. His erection jumped in agreement. Crazy. He clenched his jaw and pulled her tight against him and willed himself to chill.

After they'd both calmed, Olivia reluctantly eased off and rolled onto her back. She reached for his hand and he wrapped his strong fingers around her palm.

"You okay?" he asked.

"Mmm-hmm. You?"

"Yeah." He squeezed her hand. "I was thinking about what you said last night."

"Humph, that bourbon did a number on me. What did I say?"

Connor turned his head toward her. "You said that you do what you do to prove your worth, show that you're of value." He felt her shrinking. "Don't. Don't turn away." He turned on his side to face her. "There's nothing that you have to prove to me, Olivia. Nothing. I want you to trust me, to believe that what we have is special. It's personal — between us — and not for the world to know."

Her doe-brown eyes glistened with unshed tears. One escaped and slid down her cheek. "I want that," she said. Her voice cracked with emotion. "I want to know that I matter to someone, that I wasn't just a thing to be gotten rid of."

"Oh, *cher.*" He pulled her to him and held her tight. He kissed the top of her head, stroked her back. "You matter to me." His gaze grazed her face. He caressed her cheek. "More than you could imagine."

Her bottom lip trembled.

He adjusted his position so that he was above her. "Look at me."

Her eyes settled on his face.

"I love you, Olivia."

Olivia's eyelids fluttered; her lips parted ever so slightly. She felt a kind of warmth spread from her belly. Her heart began to pound. She couldn't catch her breath. She'd never heard those words from anyone before. "I . . . Connor . . ." Tears sprang from her eyes. "No one has ever loved me."

His heart nearly broke with the weight of her pain. He squeezed her to him. "Someone loves you now. *I do.* I love you, Olivia." He held her and rocked her and whispered to her, soothed her until her cries had subsided.

Olivia curled into his embrace, wanting to get so close that she became a part of him. Love. It was an emotion that always eluded her. As she'd grown up and moved from place to place, family to family, she'd found a way to strip herself of emotion, surround herself with an invisible barrier so that she wouldn't become attached. There were times that she was so hungry for love that she grew ill. The doctor prescribed vitamins. There wasn't a pill for what she needed. And now someone was here to love her, had professed his love for her. Finally, the one thing that she'd longed for had arrived, and she had no experience on how to return it.

Chapter 19

Connor knew that Olivia was deeply shaken by his admittance of love. It was still incredibly hard for him to fathom that one could go through life without being surrounded by love. He could only imagine how being a foster child had shaped her life and perception of the world and who she was in it. Unfortunately, not much of it was good. It would take time for her to accept what he'd said and, more important, to believe what he'd said. Her entire life of relationships was built on a temporary and no-commitment foundation. But he was a patient man. He would wait however long it took.

"Hey," said a whispered voice behind him.

Connor looked at Olivia's reflection in the bathroom mirror. "Hey, sleepyhead." He stretched his jaw and slowly glided the shaver across the morning stubble.

She leaned against the door frame. "I kind

of like the after-five look."

He took a quick glance over his shoulder and grinned. "Oh, yeah. I'll keep that tomorrow." He finished up, splashed water on his face and toweled off.

Olivia smiled at the reveal. "Not bad."

"Thanks." He walked up to her, rested his hands on her hips and took her mouth in a quick, sweet kiss. He brushed his thumb across her bottom lip. "I put on coffee."

She looped her arm through his. "After a quick shower, I'll fix breakfast."

"No argument from me."

Connor toyed with his coffee cup and mulled over how best to spring the news on Olivia about the book. He didn't want to give her false hope, but he couldn't keep it from her. She was a highly skilled researcher. If there was evidence one way or the other about her origins in the pages of that book, Olivia would find it.

Olivia spooned the scrambled eggs onto a platter along with the grilled Italian sausages. "Not my finest effort," she said lightly. She put the platter in the center of the table. "But it's guaranteed to hit the spot. I saw some OJ in the fridge. Want some?"

"Sure." He watched her move around his

living space with the ease of someone who belonged there. Even as heavy as things had become between him and Adrienne, he'd rarely had her stay at his place. He could probably count the times on one hand. It never occurred to him until now why. He didn't want to share his space, his sanctuary, with anyone else. He lifted the coffee mug to his lips and stared at Olivia above the rim. Now he did.

"What?" Olivia said with a curious grin when she caught him staring. "Egg on my face?"

"No. Nothing like that. Just looking."

She sat down opposite him. "Something's on your mind. I can feel it. What is it?"

He pushed out a breath. "Stay right here." He got up and went into the living room. He went to the bookcase and took the book from between a Jeffery Deaver thriller and a journal on modern restoration. For a moment he felt the weight of it in his hands, then went back to the kitchen. Gingerly he set it down on the table between them.

"What's that?"

He told her about running into Ms. Farmer and coming across the book in her attic. "I don't know what it means or if it means anything at all but I couldn't let it go." He pushed the book toward her.

The badly faded embossed lettering on the front cover was barely legible. She could just make out "Dayton-Gray." Her gaze flew to Connor.

Her fingers trembled ever so slightly as she opened the book. Much of it was hard to make out without the proper equipment. The pages were stiff from water and smoke damage and the words and images were faint as ghosts. And then she turned a page and a picture of what could easily have been her stared back at her.

Olivia's breath caught in her chest. She blinked, stared, peered closer. She tenderly ran her hand across the image and the name below. Ellen Dayton. The resemblance was remarkable.

But as remarkable as it was, it didn't make sense until she read a bit further about the Dayton-Gray line. The last entry was about the great-granddaughter of Ellen. Her name was Leslie. The entries and story ended there. The subsequent pages were totally destroyed. The name Leslie Gray was the only identifier on Olivia's birth certificate, which she'd had to fight to obtain. But as hard as she'd tried, and despite all the resources that she'd used, she'd never been able to uncover anything beyond the name Leslie Gray — until now.

Trancelike, Olivia closed the book and rested her hands on the cover. "I . . . I'm not sure what it all means." She swallowed. "But maybe now I have a new place to start." She shook her head. "It couldn't be . . . could it?"

Connor stretched his hand across the table and covered hers. "It could be the answer that you've been searching for or it could be a twisted coincidence." He squeezed her hands. "Whatever way it goes, I'm not going anywhere."

Olivia sniffed. "Thank you," she whispered.

Connor dropped Olivia off at home with the promise to see her later. He had a lot of catching up to do at the site.

Before Connor was fully out of the driveway Olivia was on her cell phone scrolling through her contact list. She had a friend, Naomi Hailey, who worked for the National Endowment for the Arts, one of the agencies helping to fund the project that she was working on. Olivia was hoping that Naomi could work her magic and come up with some background on Leslie Gray, now that she finally had something more to go on than a name.

"Olivia, good to hear from you. How are

things?"

"Good. Busy. Listen, I have a favor to ask."

"Sure. If I can."

"I need you to see if you can find any information on a Leslie Gray. She is related to Ellen Dayton of Dayton Village."

"Really? Okay. I'll look into what we have on file and get back to you as soon as I can."

"Thanks, Naomi."

Olivia's nerves twanged with every breath she took as she waited for Naomi to call back. The chances of her being related to Leslie Gray were remote at best. But stranger things had happened. She must have walked a country mile and then some by the time Naomi called back.

"Did you find anything on Leslie Gray?" she spouted on the heels of hello.

"Well, not exactly. There's nothing on her at all other than her mother is Constance Dayton Gray. Her I have information on."

Olivia's heart galloped at racetrack speed. "I'm listening. No, wait. Let me get a pen."

"Relax, I'm going to email everything to you. Just a little heads-up. She lives in Harlem on what was once Strivers Row. I'll send over the phone number, as well."

Olivia could barely get out the words *thank you.* She disconnected the call, bit down on her lip as if that would somehow contain the maelstrom of anxiety that was zipping through her. She hurried over to her computer and clicked on her email account. The seconds ticked by while she waited for the email from Naomi to arrive.

Finally the telltale *bing.* Olivia clicked on the email and opened it. She was so nervous she had to read everything twice before it made sense to her. Before she did anything totally crazy she called Connor, who told her to simply take a breath and do what she did best — dig for information.

"Call her," he urged. "Explain the project that you're working on and see what she says."

"Right. Right," Olivia said. "Okay. I'll call."

"Don't forget to breathe," he teased. "Call me after."

"I will."

Olivia squeezed the phone in her hand, said a silent prayer and then tapped in the number that Naomi had given her.

The phone rang and rang and her pulse raced and raced and then someone answered.

"Gray residence."

"Yes. Hello. My name is Olivia Gray. Dr. Olivia Gray, and I hoped to reach Constance Gray."

"Speaking."

Her knees wobbled. Slowly she lowered herself into an available chair. "Ms. Gray. You don't know me, but I'm an anthropologist working on the restoration of Dayton Village in Sag Harbor."

There was a long moment of silence.

"I . . . Oh, my. Someone called months ago and asked permission . . . and you are the one working on it."

"Yes. I am."

"How can I help you? None of the family has been there in decades. I can't imagine what's left."

"Oh, Ms. Gray, you would be amazed. We've found some of the original freedom papers, birth records and even schoolbooks from the early settlers." Olivia paused, took a breath. "I was hoping that you would be willing to meet with me."

"I don't know how much I can add to what you already know, but . . . of course. I'd love to see what you've discovered."

Olivia fought to contain her excitement. "Wonderful. I know this may seem rushed, but I could drive out to see you tomorrow afternoon if that works for you."

Another long pause, then the woman asked, "Will three o'clock work with your schedule?"

"Absolutely."

"Fine. Take this address."

Olivia wrote down the address and cross streets. "Thank you so much, Ms. Gray. I'll see you tomorrow at three."

"See you then, Dr. Gray. *Gray.* Curious that it would be a Gray that found a Gray."

Olivia swallowed. "Yes."

"Tomorrow then, Dr. Gray."

Olivia put the phone down. Her thoughts were spinning around in her head so fast that she couldn't latch on to one long enough for it to make sense. What if? What if her journey's end was only a few hours away?

The ringing of the phone startled her back to reality. She snatched it up from the table.

"Connor, I called. I spoke to Constance Gray," she burst out before he had a chance to say a word. "And I'm going to see her tomorrow."

"Whoa. You spoke with her?"

"Yes. I told her who I was and what I was doing, and when I asked if I could meet with her, she agreed. Tomorrow at three."

"Baby, I'm happy for you. But keep your feet on the ground. This could be something or it could be nothing at all."

Olivia blew out a breath. "I know." She waited a beat. "That's why I want you to come with me."

"Whatever you need."

Her insides smiled. "See you when you get off?"

"I'll think about it," he joked. "Around eight."

"See you."

Olivia flopped onto the couch and stretched out her legs. She closed her eyes as a sudden wave of exhaustion wilted her limbs — the aftereffect from the rush of adrenaline. She knew she needed to stay focused. Although this was without a doubt a personal quest, she had to keep at the forefront that it was also her job. This family was part of the history of Dayton Village, and no matter what else might happen, Olivia was responsible for gathering and documenting the information. She could not allow her personal issues to cloud her professionalism.

Tomorrow could not arrive fast enough.

CHAPTER 20

For most of the two-hour drive into Manhattan, Connor held Olivia's hand. He listened to her fears and questions. He allayed her concerns, answered what questions he could and put out the fire of doubt.

"If she's agreed to see you, I'm sure she is just as curious to find out about her family. The thing you have to do is remember that they are part of your research, no matter which way it turns out. And if it happens that they're your relatives, that's the extra bonus."

Olivia nodded. She'd done countless interviews with relatives, friends and the general public as part of her research. She knew the drill. But this time was different. She felt it in her soul. The key would be not to go in there demanding the answers that she wanted, but opening the doors for Constance Gray to walk through on her own.

With fifteen minutes to spare, Connor pulled the car onto 138th Street and Adam Clayton Powell Jr. Boulevard. The majestic homes that made up Strivers Row had been built between 1889 and 1892 by David H. King Jr. The Row was made up of light brown Italianate palazzos, redbrick neo-Georgians and Renaissance revival–style houses with beige brick and terra-cotta ornaments. They'd been off-limits to black homeowners until 1919. Soon after, some of the city's most prominent black New Yorkers — like entertainer Bill "Bojangles" Robinson and politician Adam Clayton Powell Jr. — moved in. Moving onto Strivers Row was an indication that "you had arrived."

Olivia took out her camera and photographed the stately row of town houses. Funny, in all her travels and research she'd never been to this part of Harlem. She'd seen the amazing photographs of the exteriors and the breathtaking interiors, but now she would experience them for herself.

"It's the one on the end," Olivia said, confirming the address with the information on her iPad.

Connor cruised to a stop and parallel parked into a space two doors down from Constance Gray's home. He cut the engine and turned to Olivia. "Ready?"

She expelled a shaky breath. "Yes."

He got out of the car and reached into the backseat for her bags, which held her cameras, laptop, tape and video recorders, notebook and the Dayton family journal.

Olivia took one of the tote bags and hoisted it over her shoulder. They walked toward the house and up the stoop steps to the parlor floor and the ornate entry door. Olivia took a quick look at Connor, dragged in a breath and rang the bell.

It felt as if an eternity passed before someone finally came to the door. When it opened, a woman of indeterminate age, dressed casually in a button-up beige cashmere sweater and tan slacks, was standing there. At first glance, with her very fair skin and emerald-green eyes, she could pass for white. But there was a hint of her blackness in the angle of her head and the way her full lips welcomed a kiss. For an instant her green eyes flashed and widened when she saw Olivia, but just as quickly settled back down to cool observation.

"You must be Dr. Gray." She turned her gaze and perused Connor.

"Hello. Yes, I'm Dr. Gray and this is Connor Lawson. He is working on the restoration of the buildings."

Constance seemed to hesitate, as if she was rethinking her invitation. Finally, she stepped aside to let them in.

Olivia and Connor dutifully followed Constance inside. They entered the foyer and faced a winding staircase constructed of the heavy dark wood of times gone by. The front room was to the right and they were immediately taken back fifty, sixty years to the grandeur of the sitting rooms that served as salons for the black elite, who would gather to discuss the arts, politics and race relations. The antique furnishings were the perfect touches to the cathedral ceiling, which dripped with crystal chandeliers that danced in the light like glass ballerinas. Heavy mahogany molding, gleaming hardwood floors, a working fireplace and massive mantel with a built-in mirror that rose to the ceiling all added to the historic ambience of the brownstone.

Connor was totally in his element. He was captivated by the intricate detail in the woodwork, the original molding, built-in wall sconces and the pocket doors that closed off for intimacy and opened onto an even larger room for those historic parties that were the rage of the Renaissance.

"Your home is incredible," Connor said. "You've maintained all of the original details." He turned to Constance, and she seemed to immediately soften under the spell of his smile.

"Yes. I inherited the house. It's been in the Gray family for decades. We were determined to keep it as original as we could. Of course, we've had to update the plumbing and electricity, repair the roof and such, but overall it's the way it was when it was built."

"This is a landmarked property, correct?" Of course he already knew that, but he wanted to keep her engaged, to give Olivia time to collect herself.

"Yes, it is. This entire section, 138th to 139th Streets, are designated landmarks."

"I'm sure your home must be one of the major highlights during the historic tours."

Constance giggled like a girl, and for a moment, a reflection of the young woman she once was appeared. "Oh, I don't know about all that," she said coyly. "Oh, my, where are my manners. Please, have a seat. Can I get you anything to drink?"

"No, thank you," Olivia said, the first words she'd uttered since they came in.

"Nothing for me," Connor added. He sat next to Olivia on a Queen Anne couch, complete with the scalloped back and print fabric.

Constance took a seat in a straight-backed

chair and folded her long fingers on her lap. She looked from one to the other, hesitating for a moment on Olivia. Her expression seemed to falter, then settle. "So how can I help you?"

"I was hoping to talk with you about the Dayton family, what you remember, things you may have been told by your parents and grandparents." Olivia swallowed. "Things passed along to your children."

Constance stiffened.

"What I want to do is try to piece together a timeline. I have a little information about your great-grandparents, but after the village dissolved, the history seems to be lost."

Constance linked and unlinked her fingers. "I don't have much to tell. My mother, Ellen, wasn't much of a talker," she said, with an inflection of disdain. Her features tightened. "From what I do remember, she didn't want to have anything to do with . . . her past." Constance pursed her lips.

Olivia reached for the tote that she'd set on the floor between her feet. She pulled out the Dayton family journal. "This is one of the items that was recovered. May I?" she asked, wanting permission to show it to her.

"Yes, of course."

Olivia got up and came to stand beside

Constance. She carefully opened the book to the page with Ellen on her wedding day. Olivia watched Constance's narrow nostrils flare as she stared at the photograph.

"I've never seen this photo," she said wistfully. Tenderly she touched the images. "My mother and I were never close, you see. I was . . . too dark." Her lips pursed at the sourness of the words.

Olivia held her breath and hoped for more revelations.

"If you were the right color, you could 'pass' back then. My father could pass and did. He built a life as a white man. He married my mother and I guess they thought they could keep up the charade — until I was born." She handed the book back to Olivia. "So you see, I don't have much to tell."

Olivia held the book to her chest. "Would you like to see some of the other items that I recovered?"

Constance blinked away the past and looked up at her. Again that instant of shock registered in the woman's eyes. "Yes, I would."

Olivia retrieved her bag and moved one of the side chairs next to Constance. She took out the plastic container that held the freedom papers, photographs and some of the schoolbooks.

Constance was totally immersed and fascinated as Olivia patiently explained what each item was, where she'd found it and its significance. She powered up her computer and turned on the PowerPoint program that showcased the array of photographic images that she'd taken of the site and the progress that was being made on the restoration.

Halfway through, they heard the front door open, and moments later a woman who had to be close to a very spry eighty-something appeared in the doorway. She stopped cold as if she'd seen a ghost, and her café au lait complexion darkened. She gasped in alarm, but quickly recovered. "Connie, I didn't know you had company," she said, trying to cover her faux pas.

Connor stood when she entered the room.

"Ann, this is Dr. Olivia Gray and Connor Lawson. They are both working on the restoration of Dayton Village. Ann Holmes is my father's sister. We share the house together."

Connor crossed the room and extended his hand. "Nice to meet you, Ms. Holmes."

Ann tried to focus on Connor, but her attention kept drifting back to Olivia.

"Dr. Gray was showing me what they've

accomplished. She has photographs."

"Oh . . . may I?" The woman crossed to where Constance was sitting.

Olivia gave up her seat and offered it to Ann Holmes. She stepped closer to Connor and looked to him to get a gauge on what he was thinking. He lifted his chin and raised a brow to encourage her to take the next step.

"Ms. Gray, I have another reason for coming here today."

Both women looked up from the items in front of them.

Olivia swallowed down her apprehension. "I think I may be related to you . . . to the Dayton-Gray family."

Constance's cheeks flushed red. She gripped the sides of the chair. "Simply because we have the same name is no earthly reason to believe that we could in any way be related. There are thousands of Grays. Should I entertain the idea that we are all related? In your research, Doctor, did you uncover that we are a very wealthy family?"

"Connie!" Ann gasped.

"Ms. Gray, I assure you money is not the reason. I'm quite comfortable financially. I . . . never knew my parents." Connor placed a reassuring hand on her arm. "I was given up at birth. I've spent the better part of my life trying to forget my unfortunate past or trying to explain it. This has been as close as I've ever come to maybe, just maybe, finding out who I am." Her eyes glistened with tears. "I'm sorry to have taken up your time." She sniffed and proudly lifted her chin. "I'm sure The Institute and the NEA will be in touch when the work is completed."

She collected the items on Ann's lap and returned them to the container and tote. She wanted to run away screaming. Her face was so hot with anger and shame that she felt as if she was on fire. She had to get out of there. She nearly tripped over Connor in her rush to get to the door.

Ann followed them. "I think you may be right," she whispered as Olivia crossed the threshold.

Olivia and Connor stopped. They both turned back to her.

Ann's lips were tightly pressed together. She nodded her head. "Take my number and call me tomorrow morning," she said softly.

Olivia, stunned, at least had the presence of mind to take out her cell phone. She tapped in Ann's phone number. "Thank you."

"No promises." She closed the door.

Olivia pressed her hand to her chest as she descended the stairs. "Connor . . ." she said, her voice lifting in question.

"I know, babe. I know. But we can't get ahead of ourselves. One thing at a time. Look, instead of driving all the way back, let's find a hotel in the city. This way . . . if anything . . . after the call, if we need to we can come right back . . ." He opened the passenger side door.

She eagerly bobbed her head. "Oh, Connor." She looked up at him, her eyes shimmering with hope and fear.

He placed his hands on her waist. "Whatever happens, I'm here." He gave her a quick reassuring kiss.

"You need to accept the truth once and for all, Constance. You've buried your head in the sand for decades," Ann scolded.

Constance held her ground. "That young woman simply wants to get her hands on the Dayton-Gray money!"

"Constance. Stop it, just stop it." Ann softened her tone and went to stand in front of her niece. "I know how difficult it was for you all those years, feeling that you were not wanted or loved. So you spent your life trying to be worthy, belonging to all the right organizations, attending the right schools, living here . . . All this . . ." she added, spreading her arms expansively. "None of that will change how your parents made you feel. But, Connie, you passed your secret shame onto your daughter. That's why she could never tell you. And that secret has come home to roost."

Constance slowly lost the stiffness in her back and eased herself into a chair.

"Everything that's done in the dark will come to light. It always does. That young woman needs to know the truth, and you need to face it. We all do."

Soft tears slid down Constance's smooth cheeks. She reached out her hand and her aunt Ann took it.

Chapter 21

Olivia barely slept. Every few minutes it seemed she was waking to look at the clock. The night dragged on and her racing thoughts gave her no rest. In the morning, one way or the other, she would find out what she'd been searching for all her life. Would knowing really change her? Would she feel different? What if she wasn't part of the family and this was all one big crazy co-incidence? Stranger things had happened.

"You're going to be exhausted if you don't get some sleep," Connor said, his own voice husky with sleep. "Come here." He gathered her close to him.

She rested her head on his chest and the soothing, steady rhythm of his heartbeat began to settle her.

"I can only imagine what you are going through, *cher,*" he whispered into the night. "But no matter what, you are going to come out of this okay. You know why?"

"No . . ."

"Because I love you. I love you and I will be there to hold your hand, to wipe away tears of sadness or joy. You're not alone in the world anymore, Liv. I'm here. And it's not temporary. I'm staying."

Something inside her shifted as if the world had slid momentarily off its axis. She felt full and light and happy and scared all at once. Desperately she wanted to crack open the door and take a step out onto the foundation of possibility. But underneath her the ground was still unsteady, and even with Connor's words of love and his vow to stay, the fear that had been so much a part of who she was, sewn into the fabric of her existence, was still there. She couldn't reach the knob of hope to turn it and push the door open.

Connor lightly kissed the top of her head. "Try to rest."

Olivia closed her eyes and the cocooning comfort of Connor finally lulled her to sleep.

The sound of rushing water eased into Olivia's slumber. When she opened her eyes she was surprised to see that it was after eight in the morning. She'd actually rested. She pushed the covers aside, stretched and stood up. Connor was in the shower and the smell of coffee was in the air. He'd put on a pot while she'd slept.

She smiled at the tiny gesture. He was crazy amazing in every way imaginable. Any woman would be a fool not to love Connor Lawson. Was she a fool? *Did* she love him and simply did not know it because she couldn't recognize it? She knew that she wanted to be with him, talk with him, go to bed and wake up with him. She was a better person with him and because of him. He made her happy on every level. He challenged her intellectually and he was solidly his own man. He was gorgeous, sexy, funny, hardworking and, best of all, he loved her. She knew that. And she also knew that she would come apart at the seams if he was not in her life.

Her heart began to race and her stomach felt so funny. The pulse in her temple pounded. She pressed her hand to her chest as she suddenly couldn't breathe. She pushed up from the bed and walked to the bathroom. Her hand shook ever so slightly as she reached for the knob. She turned it and stepped in.

The room swirled with steam almost as if it were a dreamscape. Connor, behind the curtain, hummed an offbeat tune.

Olivia stepped closer. The emotions that raced through her were so overwhelming that she could barely move. She slowly slid the curtain aside. Connor turned, not startled in the least, but easy and confident as he looked at her with a warm inviting smile.

"Hey, babe."

"I . . . I love you." She swallowed. Her heart pounded. The dam inside her burst.

Connor's eyes darkened. He held out his hand to her. "Come in and tell me again."

She tore off her robe, a giddy kind of joy zipping through her veins. She stepped into the shower.

Water rushed over them.

"Tell me again, Olivia Gray."

She looked up at him as water poured over her face, masking the tears of joy that rolled down her cheeks. "I love you, Connor Lawson. I love you."

He leaned down and covered her mouth. The kiss was raw and passion filled and sweet and solid. He held her tight, pressed her back against the wall. He stroked her body, planted kisses, set her skin on fire and readied her for him. "Say it again," he groaned as he cupped her breasts, taunted her nipples and found his way inside her.

Olivia cried out in pleasure, "I love you. Yesss . . ."

■ ■ ■ ■

It was a little after ten in the morning. They'd ordered room service and were in bed watching one of those judge shows.

"Do you think it's too early to call?" Olivia took a bite of her toast.

"A little. Why don't you give it another hour?"

"Okay." She wiped her mouth with the cloth napkin. "You know what?"

"Probably not," he teased. He sipped his orange juice.

"I'm going to be okay. No matter what happens."

"I know you will."

"I didn't feel that way before."

He looked at her. "What changed?"

"You. Well . . . me. But you changed me."

He grinned. "Hmm, sounds like Jedi-mind-trick woman talk."

She playfully swatted him with her napkin. "You know what I mean."

His eyes widened cynically. "Um, of course I do. You were perfectly clear."

Olivia huffed. "I opened the door. I stepped out and I didn't fall. You didn't let me fall. I've never loved anyone, not really. I've never told anyone that I loved them."

She blinked and looked away. "Until you. And I feel . . . whole for the first time in my life." She lowered her head as her eyes filled with tears.

Connor put his tray aside and slid closer to her. He lifted her chin with the tip of his finger. "As long as I have a breath in me, you will always feel whole. Always," he added softly. He winked to lighten the heavy emotional moment. "Now eat up, woman, so you'll have the strength you'll need when I ravish you."

"Well . . ." Connor waited.

Olivia put down the phone. She looked at him with a mixture of fear and elation. "They want to meet this afternoon at five."

He beamed. "That's great news."

"There would be no need to meet if there wasn't something substantial to say," she said, a note of hope in her voice.

"More than likely not."

She pressed her palms together almost in a posture of prayer. "Five hours."

"Yeah. Since I'm in town and have some time, I want to take care of a few things, visit a couple of my suppliers. If I leave now I'll be back in plenty of time to go with you."

Olivia looked at him curiously for a moment. She shrugged lightly. "Okay."

"I shouldn't be more than an hour."

"I'll keep myself busy. I have reports to review."

He kissed the top of her head. "See you soon."

Olivia watched him walk out the hotel room door. She had a strange feeling in the pit of her stomach, but then it went away.

Connor walked to the corner and hailed a Yellow Cab. "Fifty-seventh and Park," he told the driver. He sat back and played all the possible scenarios in his head. It could go easy or ugly. The choice was not his. But today was the day of reckoning, settling all the business of the past one way or another.

The drive was only fifteen minutes. He paid his fare, got out and pushed through the glass doors of the office building. The Institute took up all twenty-five floors. When he walked into the lobby he had to stop at the security desk. Since 9/11 all the office buildings in Manhattan had instituted several levels of security before you could enter. He was asked for a photo ID, which they kept until he came back down; he had to sign in and then they called up to Reception to announce him. He was given a visitor's patch to wear on his shirt.

Connor got on the elevator to the twentieth floor. Once there, the elevator dinged and the doors swooshed open. He walked over to the receptionist, who sat behind a wide U-shaped desk, and gave his name.

"If you'll have a seat, someone will come and get you in a few minutes."

Connor walked over to the row of leather chairs and sat down. He picked up a magazine from the glass table and thumbed through it, not really seeing anything on the pages.

"Mr. Lawson?"

He looked up. A young woman, no more than twenty and dressed all in black, was in front of him. He stood.

"If you'll come with me, I'll take you to the meeting room."

Connor followed her down a short hallway and around a corner. The young woman opened a door. "Dr. Randall will be right with you."

"Thank you." Connor walked inside, took in the room, which was more library than meeting room. One entire wall, from floor to ceiling, was lined with books on restoration, research, journals on the great findings of the world. He would be in heaven if he had the time to go through the amazing collection.

"Mr. Lawson."

Connor turned. Victor Randall was as pressed and polished as he'd been the last time they'd met. He shifted his tie and closed the door.

"What can I do for you?"

"Nothing. I came here to clear the air once and for all." Connor took a step toward Victor. "That crap you pulled on Olivia was beneath even you. But let's get this straight. Olivia deserves the job. You know that, and trying to use me and my relationship with her was slimy at best." He stepped closer and saw a muscle in Victor's cheek jump. "You're going to see to it that the position is hers if she wants it," Connor said, his voice low and even. "And if she doesn't want it, you are going to make sure that her contract gets renewed anyway. You're going to apologize to her for the shit you pulled and you are never, as long as you live and breathe, going to bother her again."

Victor frowned. "You can't come in here and order me around, step in for your girlfriend —"

Connor was in his face before Victor could finish his sentence. They were nose to nose. "Don't underestimate me, Victor. I will make it my personal business to make your life impossible to live. I will use my name, my resources and my family fortune to bring you to your knees. You won't be able to get a job at the local car wash. And let's be clear — this is not a threat. I'm telling you that *is* what will happen." He took a step back and stared the man in the eye. "Are we clear?"

Victor's mouth moved but he couldn't seem to get the words out.

"I can't hear you."

"We're clear," he managed to say.

Connor clapped him on the arm. "Good. Glad to hear it, Victor. Hopefully, we won't have to revisit this conversation." He brushed by him. "Have a good day."

CHAPTER 22

"Hey," Connor called as he walked into the hotel room.

Olivia was curled on the couch in the sitting room, working on her laptop. "Hey, yourself. Take care of everything with your vendors?"

"Yeah," he said, and joined her on the couch. "What are you doing?"

"Nothing much. Going over some notes."

"How about we take a walk and maybe find someplace to have a late lunch, then come back and get ready to head over?"

Olivia hopped up from the couch as if she'd been hit with a zap gun. "I thought you'd never ask. I'm starved and I'm getting antsy sitting here."

They found a great bistro about three blocks away from the hotel on Amsterdam Avenue. Seated at the window, they ordered lunch and Connor entertained Olivia with his spot-on observations of the people who walked by. Before Olivia realized it, two hours had passed and she hadn't stressed once about the upcoming meeting. Connor knew exactly what he was doing.

She hooked her arm through his as they walked back to the hotel. "Will you always know what I need?" she softly asked.

He looked down into her questioning eyes. "That's the plan."

"No matter what happens . . . we'll deal with it," Connor said. He squeezed her hand.

Olivia nodded, tugged in a breath and rang the bell. Moments later Ann came to the door.

"Thank you for coming," she said. She stepped aside to let them in. "We're in the front room." She shut the door and let them into the formal front room.

Constance was seated next to her husband. But Olivia's gaze landed and stayed on the middle-aged woman who was seated near the window with a handsome man at her side. Olivia's heart hammered in her chest. She saw herself reflected in the woman's features the same way she did in the face of Ellen Dayton, right down to the tiny cleft in her chin.

Ann made the introductions. "Olivia Gray, Mr. Lawson, this is my niece's husband, Phillip." She then turned to the woman by the window. "And this is Constance's daughter, Leslie, and her husband, Martin."

Olivia couldn't breathe.

"Please sit," Ann said to Olivia and Connor.

"We had a very difficult night," Constance began. "Digging into the past, turning up secrets, lies and pain, is never easy. But it's time for the secrets to be told." She looked at her daughter.

Olivia caught a glimpse of Leslie covering her mouth as if to stifle a cry. Leslie's husband pressed his hand on her shoulder.

"When I was away at college . . . Spelman . . ." She glanced at her husband, who gave her a nod of encouragement. "I thought I was in love and . . . I had a baby." She swallowed. "I hid it from my family, stayed away for the holidays and made excuses why I couldn't come home for visits." She lowered her head. "I knew . . . I believed that my family would never accept me or my child. It wasn't what the Daytons did." She straightened. "I had the baby." She looked directly at Olivia. "Giving you away . . . was the hardest thing I've ever done. Every day of my life I have regretted it, and at the same time lived in fear that . . . this day would come."

"The only person who knew was me," Ann confessed. "I made all the arrangements, and with the Dayton name and money, I was able to keep it all hush-hush."

"The only thing I could give you was the name Gray," Leslie said in a weak voice. She blinked back tears, to no avail. "Your father's name was Martin Fields. He didn't want to deal with me or a child. I found out that he was killed in a car accident the year after you were born."

Olivia sat transfixed. A maelstrom of emotions whipped through her — anger, elation, confusion and hurt. She'd been given away, tossed aside with no more than a last name, because her birth would have tarnished the Dayton-Gray name? And she'd had a biological father who didn't want her, either. So simple, and at the same time it was so incredibly horrid.

"Do you have any idea what your decision has done to me?" Olivia asked, her voice breaking with each word. "The loneliness, moving from one home to another, never being sure if anyone would ever care about me? The questions that constantly ran through my head. Why? What was wrong with me? Why was I not worthy to be loved?"

"I can never make up for what I did. I was scared. I was young." Leslie shook her head sadly. "I am so very sorry, Olivia. From the depths of my soul, I'm sorry."

"It was more my fault than Leslie's," Constance said. "I put all those false ideals in her head because of what I'd been through, how I'd been treated in my own family. I never wanted that for Leslie. I wanted her to be educated, accepted, marry well." She lowered her head in shame.

The room sank into silence as the confessions and recriminations took center stage.

Olivia drew in a breath and slowly stood. She looked at this family that she'd spent her whole life longing for, and realized how much of her life she'd wasted. She had the answers that she needed, and the funny thing was it no longer mattered. She turned to Connor, a shadow of a sad smile on her lips. "Let's go."

Connor took her hand.

"Olivia," Leslie called out.

Olivia stopped and looked at the woman who had given her birth, and saw her reflection in another twenty years.

"I'm sorry."

"So am I." She walked out with Connor at her side.

CHAPTER 23

Olivia was quiet on the drive back to Sag Harbor. Connor allowed her the mental and emotional space that she needed. She would talk when she was ready, and he'd be there to listen. He'd thought about taking her to her house but decided that she needed to be taken care of today. He made the turn that led to his house.

"Why don't you relax, turn on some music, and I'll fix us a drink. I think we could use it." He smiled warmly at her.

Olivia mindlessly followed Connor's instructions, then plopped down on the couch, pressed her fist against her lips and stared off into space.

Connor brought her a short glass of bourbon, which she drank without a word. He took a seat opposite her.

"I'm going to be all right, you know."

"I know."

She sighed. "I don't know what I was hoping for, some storybook revelation and ending." She shook her head.

"Not much in life is what we expect."

"That's certainly true."

"What do you want to do . . . about what you know?"

She looked at him. "I want to move on with my life. The questions have finally been answered. I thought I would feel some kind of connection once I knew who my mother was. But I don't."

"What do you feel?"

"Hmm, hard to put into words . . . but satisfied. Satisfied that, despite the decisions that were made about my life, I made a life for myself. A good one, a life that I'm proud of. Not having me in their lives all these years was their loss. Growing up in that rarified air would have made me someone other than who I am." She smiled, a genuine smile. "And I like me."

Connor's dark eyes sparkled. "I kinda like you, too."

"And you know what else?"

"What?"

"I'm starved. What does a girl have to do to get a meal around here?"

Connor rose from his seat. The corner of his mouth lifted. "I can think of all kinds of things."

Olivia reached up and grabbed him by his shirt and pulled him toward her. He braced his hands on either side of her head.

"Kiss me," she said.

"With pleasure."

"I need to go to my place," Olivia said the following morning. "I have to change clothes and then I want to go into town and pick up a few things. I'm fixing dinner tonight," she said, and winked.

"Sounds good to me." Connor zipped his jeans.

"I have a list of people who I would like to interview. Based on the census there are at least a dozen families here whose history goes back several generations. When I get back to my place I'll make some calls to set up times."

"I'll drop you off on my way. I have a full day myself."

When Olivia crossed her threshold she was suddenly overcome with the events of the previous day. She'd put on a good face for Connor because she didn't want him to worry about her. But her insides were raw. Yes, she believed the things she'd said and the position that she'd taken, but it didn't stop her from feeling the unimaginable hurt.

She was, if nothing else, a scientist. She was logical, methodical, and she knew that this was all part of the process. All she could do was move through it. That would take time, but she knew she would be okay.

She put her things down and went into the kitchen just as her cell phone rang. She looked at the name on the illuminated face and groaned. But after what she'd been through there was nothing that Victor could do or say to make it worse.

"Hello, Victor."

"Olivia." He cleared his throat. "I want to apologize for my very unprofessional behavior during the meeting. It was out of place and uncalled for."

Olivia nearly fell into the chair. Her mouth opened but nothing came out.

"I've said as much to the staff as well, but I wanted you to hear it from me."

Any minute she was expecting someone to jump out from behind a door and say that she was being punked.

"And as far as the appointment to the director's position, it's yours if you still want it. No strings attached."

"I don't know what to say."

"Say that you'll accept my apology and that you will at least think about the position."

"What brought all of this on, Victor?"

Empty space hung between them for a moment. "I had a crisis of conscience. Let's leave it at that."

"Thank you for calling. Thank you for the apology, and I'll think about the job."

"That's all I ask." He paused. "How is the work coming?"

She quickly brought him up to date on the progress and her plans.

"Keep me in the loop. My new position is on hold. I told them I wanted to stay on at The Institute until my job was filled."

"No pressure," she said with a halfhearted chuckle.

"Think about it and get back to me. Give it some thought. Take care, Olivia."

"Thanks. You, too." Slowly she put the phone down, still stunned by the conversation. An "attack of conscience." She would have never thought that Victor had a conscience. She shook her head in bemusement. Whatever. She wasn't going to let his newfound soul dominate her thoughts. She still had work to do.

"You'll never guess what happened today," Olivia said as she lay in bed that night with Connor.

"Probably not, but I can guess that you're

going to tell me."

She nudged him in the side. "Victor called me."

Connor shifted his reaction to neutral. "Yeah, what did he want this time?"

"He called to apologize. Can you believe that? And he offered the job to me."

"Really? What brought all that on?"

"I have no idea. He said he had an 'attack of conscience.' "

Connor bit back a smile, thankful for the dark. "Stranger things have happened."

"I suppose. Do you think I should try to . . . have a relationship with my mother?" she asked, totally switching gears.

"I think that you need some time to digest everything. I think that you both deserve to know each other, if it's what you both want. That's your family, with all the bruises and scars. Like so many other families, yours has dirty laundry. But it's all out in the open now. You don't have to make a decision one way or the other. When the time is right, you'll know what to do."

Olivia curled closer to him. "Thank you," she whispered.

"For what?"

"For being there for me."

"I'm here because I love you."

She tilted her face toward his. "I know."

■ ■ ■ ■

The work on the homestead was coming into the final stretch. All the foundation work had been done and the interiors were nearly complete. In another week everything would be finished, as long as they stayed on schedule. When one walked onto the property it was no longer a wasteland of dilapidated buildings and rutted land. The buildings that had been completed inside and out were being outfitted with furnishings. The dirt roads were smoothed; the shrubbery, grass and trees were pruned. Flowers bloomed. You could almost see and hear the original inhabitants murmuring their approval. There was a rocker that sat on the porch of one of the houses, and every now and again it would rock all by itself. Rather than alarming her, it always made Olivia smile.

Olivia worked tirelessly documenting every step and photographing the process of the restoration. She'd interviewed five families and had acquired an enormous amount of information that included oral testimonies, family journals, letters and photographs that would all become part of the archival collection. As she watched the progress she was continually moved by the realization that she had roots here. Part of her history was on this land where her ancestors had once walked, and it filled her with a sense of pride that she'd never before experienced.

She'd eventually decided not to take the director's job. Being in the field, doing the real research, was who she was. She'd wither away behind a desk. She knew that now. Victor was disappointed, but he said that he understood and wished her well, and would make sure that her contract was renewed if that was what she wanted.

It had been three months since she'd met her family. It didn't sting quite as much and she was sure that eventually she would return the calls that Leslie made to her. But for now, she wasn't ready.

Finally the day came and all the hard work paid off. Connor, Jake and his crew, along with Olivia, took a tour of the finished job. It was beyond amazing. It was akin to taking a walk back in time. There was no detail that was left undone.

"You should be so proud of this work," Olivia said, slipping her arm around Connor's waist.

"You're a big part of this. I hope you know

and accept that."

"I do."

Connor turned to her. He took her hand and lowered himself down on one knee. All the men grew quiet. Olivia's heart raced. Her eyes widened.

"That's what I hope you'll say when I ask you . . . Do you want to share my life with me, be my friend and confidante, my lover —" which drew snickers from the guys "— my wife?" He reached in his pocket and held a sparkling diamond in the palm of his hand.

Olivia's eyes were so filled with tears and her throat was so tight with emotion that she could barely get the two words out. "I do."

A roar went up from the crew and, mysteriously, bottles of champagne began to appear. Connor slid the ring onto her finger, swept her into his arms and kissed her long and deep, to the cheers of the men.

CHAPTER 24

On the surrounding land of the homestead, tents and white tables and linen dotted the emerald-green grass. Beyond, the soft roll of the ocean could be heard. The guests had begun to arrive, most of which were the entire Lawson clan right up to Connor's grandfather Clive. Devon was his best man, and Connor had to admit that his baby brother was no longer a baby and was turning heads with every step that he took. Sydni and Gabe were in attendance, along with their brand-new baby, Mia. His cousins and aunt Jacqueline and uncles were all there to share in his big day. Rafe surprisingly came alone. Desiree, Dominique and LeeAnn brought their husbands, and Maurice and Layla were in attendance.

"I'm so happy for you, my friend," Desiree said as she adjusted Olivia's veil.

"I'm so happy for me," she answered. "This past year has been a whirlwind of changes and revelations. I would have never thought when I came to Sag Harbor that I would find my past and my future here."

Desiree squeezed her hand. "You deserve it," she said softly.

There was a light knock on the door.

"Come in," Desiree called out.

The door opened and Leslie stepped in.

Olivia turned around on the stool. "I'm glad you came."

"Thank you for inviting me."

"Desi, this is my mother, Leslie Gray-Worthy."

"Oh, hello." She extended her hand. "The resemblance . . ." They could be twins right down to the cleft in their chin.

Olivia and Leslie looked at each other and shared a soft smile.

"I wanted to bring you something for your wedding day." The older woman opened her purse and took out an embroidered handkerchief and handed it to Olivia. "Something old. Your grandmother Constance gave it to me when I got married. Her mother gave it to her."

Olivia took the handkerchief. "Thank you. This means a lot."

Leslie nodded. "Well, I wish you all the happiness, Olivia." She stepped closer, leaned down and placed a light kiss on her cheek. With that she turned and walked out.

For a moment, Olivia held the handkerchief close to her chest. This was a new day, a new beginning, and maybe it was time that she let her mother be a part of it.

Olivia and Connor faced each other beneath a cloudless sky and in front of family and friends — both new and old. They listened to the reverend caution them about the ups and downs of marriage, but that together and with love they could overcome anything and should never allow the outside world to tear asunder what God had brought together.

"Olivia, I have traveled the world," Connor told her. "I have seen the seven wonders, but it was not until I met you that I wanted to put down roots. And they were wrong to only count seven, because you are the wonder that fills my life. From this day forward I give myself to you. I will be your friend, your champion, your life partner. I will love you for as long as I have breath."

"Connor, I spent my life looking behind me, looking for answers, looking for love," she answered. "When I met you I slowly began to believe that my life was not in the past but in the future — with you. You are the center of me, the pulse that runs through my veins. If you wanted to travel to the ends of the earth, I would gladly be by your side. You gave me life, you gave me what I have been searching for . . . You are my love, my love at last."

To the applause and tears of those gathered, Connor Lawson and Olivia Gray sealed their future with a kiss.

ABOUT THE AUTHOR

Donna Hill began writing novels in 1990. Since that time she has had more than forty titles published, which include full-length novels and novellas. Two of her novels and one novella were adapted for television. She has won numerous awards for her body of work. She is also the editor of five novels, two of which were nominated for awards. She easily moves from romance to erotica, horror, comedy and women's fiction. She was the first recipient of the *RT Book Reviews* Trailblazer Award, won the *RT Book Reviews* Career Achievement Award and currently teaches writing at the Frederick Douglass Creative Arts Center.

Donna lives in Brooklyn with her family. Visit her website at donnahill.com.

The employees of Thorndike Press hope you have enjoyed this Large Print book. All our Thorndike, Wheeler, and Kennebec Large Print titles are designed for easy reading, and all our books are made to last. Other Thorndike Press Large Print books are available at your library, through selected bookstores, or directly from us.

For information about titles, please call:
(800) 223-1244

or visit our Web site at:
http://gale.cengage.com/thorndike

To share your comments, please write:
Publisher
Thorndike Press
10 Water St., Suite 310
Waterville, ME 04901